ARCHIE'S HEART

A WAR STORY

P.A. GLASPY   BOYD CRAVEN III   L.L. AKERS
L. DOUGLAS HOGAN

All proceeds from the sale of this book go to the Disabled American Veterans Association

PART 1: ARCHIE

Written by P.A. Glaspy

1

Archie didn't plan on dying that day.

The day started like so many others for him. He woke up as the sun was rising. It was hard to sleep with that bright orange orb in your eyes. But he liked to get up early, which was one of the reasons why he'd set up camp facing the winter sunrise. "You only get so many days on this earth. I don't want to sleep through any of them," he'd tell his friends.

The dilapidated tent he was calling home faced the southeast in an attempt to shield him from the prevailing winter winds that usually came out of the north. It helped some, but with nighttime temps plummeting to near zero and wind chills in double-digit negatives, no one sleeping on the street was warm. Archie wasn't sleeping on the street though. He was in an old barn, falling down in some places from years of neglect, in a field behind an abandoned house on the outskirts of town. Others like him preferred to sleep in alleys and doorways in the city, but that made them susceptible to rousting by the section police with "move along, no loitering" from the more decent patrols to the "get your ass out of my sight, you filthy pile of shit" out of the asshole cops. All so the wealthy people who lived, worked, and played there didn't have to be subjected to the sight of their fellow human beings living on the streets. They didn't want to do anything about it. They just didn't want to have to see it. Archie liked to get a decent night's sleep, which he could do out there. Besides, since the invasion, too many homeless people had just disappeared, never to be seen or heard from again.

He had found the abandoned house and barn over the summer. Archie liked to walk. He got to see the area, the people, and it helped to pass the time. He found it on one of his treks out of town. He watched the place for weeks before he decided to move his things in. No one ever came out there that he could see, not the owners or any patrols. So, he moved into the barn and called it home. He chose the barn because if he was caught inside the house it could land him in jail for breaking and entering, even if it was abandoned. And jail was a bad place for the homeless. Most who went in never came out. The barn was simply trespassing. He told his closest friends about the place and invited them to join him there. They declined, not wanting to leave the city where they could usually find food and some semblance of shelter ... at least for a few hours.

It didn't really matter if no one wanted to share the place with him. Archie was content and had developed a routine. He got up, took care of his business outside the barn, then dipped some water out of the trough that he figured used to be for some sort of livestock. He kept it as clean as he could.

Archie had broken his promise to himself about the B & E and had gone into the vacant house in search of bleach to sanitize the trough right after he moved in. As he had expected, the place had been ransacked long past. It looked like the owners had vacated right after the invasion. Cobwebs and rodent droppings were the only evidence of something living having been there for a while.

He didn't expect to find any food, but that wasn't really what he was looking for then. Archie was good at foraging for food. He came from a long line of Appalachian medicine women who had taught him all the plants that were edible, along with the medicinal ones. Archie was one of the healthiest homeless people in the area. There were dried herbs hanging all over inside the barn.

Looking under the sink in the first bathroom he came to, he found the bottle of bleach he was searching for. A quick perusal of the kitchen resulted in another bleach bottle, almost full, plus a footed cast-iron Dutch oven and a large skillet. Yes, the cast-iron cooking vessels were heavy, but they were the best things to cook with over an open fire. Archie hoped the former owners would forgive his taking them and consider that he was keeping good cast iron from going to waste. He grabbed a couple of plates, a few pieces of silverware, and some old plastic cups with a faded baseball team's name on them. His kitchen was well underway.

Archie found life in the barn quiet and peaceful. He enjoyed being able to live his life the way he wanted for the most part. No one rousting him awake, no scrounging for table scraps in dumpsters like his fellow homeless people. He wasn't happy about the restrictions placed on the American people by an invading force though. He'd resigned himself to the fact that most people were more interested in being warm and fed as servants than fighting for their lost freedom. Sad, really. He had served his country, seen brothers and sisters make the ultimate sacrifice in battle, yet it seemed that was all in vain. That nation, the one they had fought so hard for, was gone now and he didn't recognize the one that was left.

He wished he could do something to change that. But he was only one man. What could he do alone?

2

He set the water to boiling in the cast-iron skillet after stoking the fire back up from the night before. It was rare that Archie ever had to actually start a fire. His fires kept coals burning all the time. He opened a pouch of roasted dandelion root, poured some onto a flat rock he had by the fire and crushed them with another long round rock by rolling it over the flat one. He placed the crushed root in a metal coffee cup and poured the boiling water over it. He let his "coffee" steep for a few minutes while he took the remaining hot water and gave himself a quick sponge bath. Once that was done, he picked up his cup, sat by the fire, and enjoyed the morning's glorious launch.

He considered himself lucky. He may not have had a house with electricity to provide light and warmth, but he also didn't have to pay rent or utilities; if that was still a thing in the new world in which he lived. He couldn't just walk into a store and buy whatever he wanted since he didn't earn any money he could use to pay for things, but the other side to that was he didn't have to put up with anyone's bullshit at a job he hated.

Guns were outlawed for anyone except the military and police, but he didn't need one to get meat. He could make a number of snares and was an excellent tracker. It was a rare occurrence when he didn't have fresh rabbit or squirrel stewing in the Dutch oven in the evening. He had also made a bow and arrows which he could use to take down a deer. He kept them out of sight, as they would be confiscated if anyone knew he had them, and the consequences of being caught with a weapon would be grave. He had found a couple of knives in the house which he had taken to the barn and stashed in a corner. He used those for cleaning game, so they were honed to a razor-sharp edge.

He thought about going deer hunting. He had some friends in town who could probably benefit from a good protein boost, and there was a small shopkeeper who took all the fresh meat Archie brought in to trade for things like flour, real coffee, and vegetables, other than the potatoes, turnips, and other root vegetables he grew outside the barn. The root veggies he could pretty much leave in the ground and pull as he needed them. With no electricity, he had no way to keep any food items that were perishable when it was hot out. In the middle of winter, he had more food-saving options than the middle of summer. Consequently, he ate very well in the winter, a time when his body needed the extra calories to stay warm. Soups and stews, thick and hearty, were usually breakfast and supper. In the summer, he turned to dried meats, berries, and wild plants, like dandelion, cattails, and poke. He wasn't crazy about the bitter taste of the poke leaves, but, hey, a guy needed his leafy greens.

Virgil, the shopkeeper, was very discreet, only offering the venison to patrons he knew would keep their mouths shut about where they got it if someone happened to stop them, check their bags, and inquire about its origins. So far, no one had been asked or even detained. He hoped it stayed that way.

3

IF EVER THERE was a war without a single bullet being fired, this one came close. The stock market crashed, banks shut and locked their doors, and China called in its loans, which of course the U.S. couldn't pay. They chose to take over the country, both government and private. Congress and the president declared the country bankrupt and pretty much gave China the keys to the kingdom. Finding out later that China had orchestrated the financial downfall of the United States didn't make the pill any less bitter to swallow. With their good friends from Russia, the invasion was underway.

Many Americans died trying to keep the country free. The president's instructions to turn in their weapons and comply with the new regime fell on deaf, well-armed ears. Veterans and citizens banded together and gave them a good fight, especially in the South, the northern part of the Midwest, and Texas. But China had been preparing for this for a long time. They knew where to send the majority of their troops, to the places that they decided would offer the heaviest resistance. The invaders didn't come out of the fight unscathed, but they were victorious. Or so they thought.

Many of the fighters retreated to the mountains or the deserts, in the hopes of living to fight another day.

The modified Communist Totalitarian society they put in place benefited the Chinese and Russians. After the collapse and subsequent occupation, there were two classes of citizens — supervisors and workers. The supervisors were made up of people who had come in from the invading countries. No Americans were supervisors, though more than one had tried to ingratiate themselves into the elite upper echelon. Former CEOs worked side by side with the guy from the mail room of what was once an industrial plant owned by them. All of the workers wore the same nondescript blue uniform. They wore boots in the winter and slip-on tennis shoes in the summer.

While no one in the cities who performed their assigned jobs went hungry, there wasn't a lot of excess in the way of food. In lieu of pay, workers were given a place to live with utilities provided, food vouchers, and department store credits. Paper money no longer existed. Once the economy collapsed, it was worthless. The only currency that had value was precious metals and gemstones — and food. The food vouchers fed the workers' families, but quite often it was barely enough to go around. Department store credits were used to purchase essentials like toilet paper or underwear and socks. The country was still there, industry was still producing — it was just being run by someone other than the U.S. government or private corporations.

Shopkeepers like Virgil were allowed to continue their trade after the collapse but had to get their store goods from the regime. They were given supplies specific to their business up front. When it was time for resupply, they turned in their food or store credits to pay for the next shipment, as well as the records they were forced to keep for every transaction. Everything was meticulously counted and controlled.

Virgil took vouchers for the official food out front and

goods in trade for the black-market stuff in the cellar. He would take a pound of salt or flour for a quarter-pound of stew meat. The staples used up less of the voucher's value than meat. Most of the livestock meat was sent overseas to China to feed their large populace. Any that was made available to the American people was highly overpriced, even though it was grown in the States. A quarter of a pound of meat could be turned into a soup that would feed a family of four as long as it had plenty of vegetables ... and water. He was always eager to receive wild game from Archie.

The homeless were another story. They were the ones who were handicapped or too sick to work, mentally or physically, or just didn't want to sacrifice what little freedom they retained for a bit of comfort. They received no vouchers, no housing, and had to beg for every scrap they got from people who had little to spare themselves. The Chinese and Russian immigrants simply ignored them or called for security, if they were accosted by one of the indigents, who would then haul the unfortunate person off to jail, many times never to be seen again. Archie tried to help them whenever he could. These were his people, some of them his brothers and sisters in arms. Archie was a combat veteran, wounded in action. A decorated hero. And he was homeless in the country he'd almost died defending.

4

Archie came back from Afghanistan in a wheelchair. The doctors said his left knee and foot would likely never work properly again. Archie had made up his mind to prove them wrong. He went to physical therapy every day, pushing his body to the limits and beyond. When he walked out with a cane, everyone applauded. He was set up in a small apartment, ready to start a new job, when it all went to hell.

He knew when the broadcasts started about China coming in to explore joint ventures with the U.S. there was something fishy about the whole thing. When his second disability check never showed up, he was sure things were going down, fast. He packed the few belongings he had into his duffel bag and limped out of his apartment. He never looked back. The pop-up tent he lived in was the same one he had when he left the city. Back then his tent was in a lot better shape. He slowly trekked to a state park, hitchhiking some of the time, but mostly just walking. He had kept the cane even after he no longer needed it and shoved it in his duffel at the last minute when he spied it leaning against the wall by the door. On the long days when he didn't get any rides, it was the difference between five miles and eight on foot.

Had his car been running, he would have been a lot further away from any major city when everything started going down, but fate had kicked him in the teeth on that one, too. His old SUV needed a new transmission, and he couldn't afford to get it fixed. When he'd lived in the city, it didn't matter. Everything he needed was within walking distance.

The state park had a campground with RV hookups, with quite a few of the spots occupied, as well as a primitive camping area right beside a lake. Archie set up his camp there. He hunted and fished and tried to mind his own business, though he did strike up friendships with a number of the other campers in the area, mostly guys who could also gather their own food. The peace lasted a couple of weeks.

He woke up one morning to the sound of a number of men stomping around outside his tent. The sun was barely past the horizon.

"Who's out there?" he asked in a raised voice.

From outside the tent a voice called back to him in clipped English heavily laden with a Chinese accent.

"You in tent! You come out now! Slow! No weapons!"

"Give me a minute to get some clothes on," he replied to the command. After donning pants and boots, he pulled his pocket knife out of his pocket and slid it under his sleeping bag. He quickly scanned the tent to make sure his pistol, rifle, and shotgun were out of sight. Satisfied, he exited the tent.

"Hands up!" The six Chinese soldiers all had automatic rifles pointed at him. Archie raised his hands and automatically locked them behind his head. The soldier who had been doing the talking said something in Chinese to the man next to him. The second man gave him a curt nod, handing his rifle to the soldier on his other side. The speaker barked at Archie.

"You no move! We search you!" The soldier who had been instructed to search Archie walked up to him and searched him thoroughly. Finding nothing, he returned to his team. The spokesman said something else to him and the man headed toward Archie's tent.

Calmly, Archie said, "Maybe if you told me what this was all about, I could help you."

"No talk until we tell you! You have weapons in tent?" the spokesman yelled.

Knowing he couldn't deny it, especially since the searcher was already opening the tent flap, Archie replied, "Yes. I have guns and knives, for self-defense, hunting, and cleaning game for food."

The leader spoke quickly in his native tongue to the searcher who replied in their own language and ducked into the tent. The spokesman turned his attention back to Archie.

"Weapons against law! No weapons for anyone but military and police. You not those! We take all! You resist, we arrest and take anyway. Stay!"

Archie closed his eyes and silently cursed the men holding guns on him, the Chinese invasion, and the drastic turn life, in general, had taken. The shotgun they were about to confiscate had belonged to his grandfather. A precious family heirloom would be dismantled and ground into scrap metal, if the rumors he'd heard were true. He gritted his teeth as the soldier came out with it, along with his .308 hunting rifle and his Smith & Wesson 40mm pistol. The guns were unceremoniously tossed on the ground, followed by two full tang, fixed blade knives and two pocket knives. Archie flinched when he heard his grandfather's shotgun skid across the gravel scattered over the area. *Sons of bitches! Sorry, Papaw.*

The leader looked around the rest of the camp. "Why you in the woods instead of in city working in factories? Where you get food?"

Archie looked the man in the eye and said, "Well, I *was* hunting in the woods here. If you take my guns, I'll have to do something else."

"Guns outlawed. You come to city. We take care of you. Give you a home, food, things you need if you work. Better there."

Archie shook his head. "No thanks. I like it out here. I'll get by."

The leader's face changed, becoming dark and fierce. He started toward Archie. Just then, four men from the RV campsites walked up.

"Everything okay, Arch?" the biggest among then called out as they continued toward the soldiers. He was carrying a baseball bat. Two of the others had ball gloves, one of them tossing a baseball up and catching it as he strode along. "We were just coming to see if you wanted get in on a game."

The leader stopped as all the soldiers turned and pointed their weapons at the approaching men. The leader yelled, "Halt! Stop right there!"

The four men stopped and held their hands up. The big man said, "Whoa. Hey, no need to get all riled up, fellas. We just want to get a game going."

The leader looked at the men and the direction they had come from. "Why you not working? How you have food, money to stay in park?"

The big man shrugged and replied, "No one's been around to collect for the camp spots. Figured since our money is no good anymore they decided not to bother. As far as food goes, we brought a bunch with us and we fish in the lake. Berries, nuts, plants you can eat — all that is right here. No one said we had to stay in town if we didn't want to, so we came out here. Is that a problem?"

The leader spoke to his men who acknowledged whatever he had said with short replies and nods. They headed toward the RV campers where the men had come from. Turning to the big man, he said in an angry tone, "We search your camp for weapons. No weapons for citizens. We protect you. You go with soldiers. Open doors. No resist!"

The big man held his hands up. "Mine's unlocked. Be my guest. I got nothing to hide." He and his friends followed the soldiers to their campers.

The leader turned back to Archie. "When you get cold and hungry, you will come to town. You will see. Not good to live outside. Not safe." With that, he gathered up Archie's guns and knives and walked away in the direction his team had gone.

Archie heard the veiled threat. He understood the patrols would be more frequent and, in all likelihood, increasingly more aggressive. Time to go.

5

AFTER THE CHINESE team of soldiers had left the campground, Archie sat down with a cup of coffee beside his modest campfire. The group of men who had come over earlier joined him. Archie looked up at the big guy.

"They get your guns, Tom?"

Tom grinned and shook his head. "Nah. That hidey hole in the floor is well built, thanks to Marcus here." He indicated the man to his left with a nod of his head. Marcus smiled and gave him a thumb's up. "They took my sacrificial knife from the drawer. The crappy one made in China." Tom smirked as the group laughed.

Archie nodded grimly. "I should have built the cache I was talking about for mine. I was going to start working on it today. Too late now."

"Sorry you lost your guns and knives, Arch, 'specially your grandpa's gun," Marcus said dejectedly. "We should have helped you get them hid."

"Don't worry about it, Marcus. I honestly didn't expect them to get out here that fast. Guess they finished harassing everyone in town already." He took a sip of his coffee and went on. "Look fellas, that team leader all but said they'll be back, and I'm betting they won't be nearly as polite. I think it's time for me to move on, maybe find something deeper in the woods or further away from town. Any of you interested in joining me?"

The men looked around at each other. Tom said, "The only problem there is we're in RVs. Not as easy to pick up and relocate as a tent. I've got my boys, Marcus has a family, Doug's wife is pregnant — it's just tougher for us."

Archie nodded and stood up. "I hear ya and I get it. I only have me to worry about. Well, I better get busy packing up." He shook each man's hand in turn. "Keep your eyes open and ears to the ground. I've got a feeling it's going to get a lot rougher for folks like us that don't want to conform to the mold."

Tom turned the handshake into a hug. "We will, Arch. Maybe we'll see each other again."

Archie smiled at him. "I'd like that. Good luck, brother." With that he started packing up his camp and was on the road an hour later. The men and their families were there to wish him well. When he got to the end of the small drive, Archie turned and waved to the small group of people he had come to care about. He hoped he would see them again.

A week or so later, Archie heard through the homeless network that a mysterious fire had consumed a small community of campers in the state park. He knew without anyone telling him it was Tom's camp. He closed his eyes and gritted his teeth, pushing down a desperate desire to do something, anything to fix his world and help bring back what it once was, but knowing he could do nothing alone. He hugged Della, who had shared the grim news, and headed out of town.

That trip that drove him further and further from the city was the one that ended in his finding the abandoned farm. Maybe it was Tom's spirit guiding him to a safer place. He liked thinking that it was. He looked heavenward and whispered, "Thanks, buddy. Rest well."

6

His hunting trip was a success. He bagged a young buck with a well-placed arrow to the heart. He hung it in the barn and quickly cleaned it. He took the hide and laid it over an old half-wall to a nearby stall that looked as if it may have been a sheep pen. He planned to work on cleaning it up later that evening. Sitting by his fire cleaning a hide was one of the things he enjoyed doing in his new solitary life. Not that he'd ever been the kind of guy who hung out with a lot of people, but he had always lived in the city, so there was constant noise from cars, electrical equipment, and people. Out there in the country, the only sounds he heard were wild life and Mother Nature. His life had changed a lot since the invasion, but he didn't think it was necessarily a bad thing. He was his own man, didn't have to worry about anybody or anything other than himself, and he liked it. He hoped the patrols didn't decide to widen their areas of operation. He had built a place that, while not heated or cooled and had no electricity, he was comfortable in. He didn't want to have to leave and start over.

He had taken parts of some old bikes he'd found and

fashioned a bike similar to a rickshaw setup. With a seat over a single wheel in the back, the handle bars were attached to the plastic basket of a former shopping cart. He had fashioned a new axle for the front and put bike wheels on each side. It had taken a lot of scrounging to get all the parts and the hardware to make it work, but once completed, it was a great way to haul things to town to trade. It took him about an hour and a half each way. It was great exercise and cut an otherwise all-day walking trip one-way down to less than half a day there and back. When he was getting ready to go, he'd load the basket with the good stuff, then cover it with items that wouldn't arouse suspicion like old clothes, blankets, that sort of thing. His bike raised a few eyebrows among the patrols, but no one had stopped to search him or the basket so far.

He cut the leg quarters, tenderloins, and ribs off the deer and put them in the basket on top of some newspapers, so they wouldn't drip blood. The small inner tenderloins he kept for himself, placing them inside the Dutch oven to be used for his supper that night. He carefully camouflaged the meat in his cart with more newspapers on top, then odds and ends of clothing, containers and other "junk" that someone would expect a homeless person to have with them. He walked around the bike checking from all angles to make sure there was no part of the meat showing. Satisfied, he donned his warmest outer wear, scooped ashes over the hot coals in his fire, and headed out.

Once he got to town, he surreptitiously checked for patrols before heading down the alley that led to the back door of Virgil's shop. He knocked softly on the door with a specific pattern in case there was anyone in the store who shouldn't see him and his offerings. Virgil knew his knock and would only answer when the coast was clear. The door opened almost immediately. Virgil leaned out with a grin.

"Man, you must be psychic or something! I just this morning sold the last of the meat you brought me last time. Come in!"

Virgil opened the door wide and grasped the front of the basket to help Archie get his bike in. It was a valuable conveyance that anybody would have liked to get his hands on. Most of the cars owned by the citizens sat in abandoned lots collecting dust and bird droppings. Gas was not a commodity the people were able to purchase. Those in power claimed that it wasn't needed by the populace. They provided mass transportation in the form of buses and subways to move folks from their homes to their workplaces and back again. Stores were within walking distance of all residences. People who had lived on the outskirts of the city were moved into an area that was close to everything they would need — or so they were told. In reality, it was to keep them in sight of the many surveillance cameras and directional microphones so that they could be monitored for subversion.

The cattle allowed themselves to be led to their new homes with promises of security and survival. They deluded themselves into thinking this was for the best and that they were actually better off now than before. They didn't have to worry about paying their bills. Everything they needed was provided for them. The credit card companies were shut down and all debt was forgiven. No one owned a house anymore, so there was no longer a need for mortgage companies. Health care was available to all at no charge. There was no actual money, so banks shut their doors. Corporate presidents, CEOs, bank managers, and the rest of the American people all worked in factories. Everything was geared toward manufacturing goods. Farms were managed by the Russians, plants by the Chinese. It was an efficient system. It was a sad excuse for life.

When they'd gotten Archie inside with his bike and

supplies, Virgil checked the alley then shut and locked the door. He waited as Archie uncovered the meat. When he saw it, he rubbed his hands together and smiled.

"Oh, that's some pretty meat you got there, Arch. What do you want for it?"

Archie pointed to one of the smaller front haunches. "That one goes to my people. Get the word out that it's here once you have it cut up. A quarter of a pound apiece should be good. Anybody acts up getting it, you let me know who and they won't be invited back. The other three ... I'll take flour, sugar, coffee, and some dry milk, if you have any. Canned vegetables will be fine. Hell, you know what I like. Oh, and some soap. Whatever you think is fair. I trust you, Virgil."

Virgil picked up the two tenderloins and one of the back legs. "Grab those other three and let's get this downstairs right away. It's so cold out it's almost frozen now. Might as well keep it that way if we can."

They took the meat down the narrow staircase that led to the basement. The front part was set up for storage. Nothing out of the ordinary, nothing to draw suspicion. What appeared to be a stabilizing bracket for a large shelf of paper products on the far wall was actually a latch to a well-hidden door. Virgil reached up with a hook, popped the latch, and slid the shelf out to reveal his "other" store.

Shelves were lined with food and other essentials, like paper and feminine products, packs of socks, gloves, toiletries, and just about anything else you might think of as a need or want. In the back of the room was cold storage. Virgil couldn't use electricity to keep perishables cold or frozen. The Coalition monitored everyone's electricity usage and an increase of any kind brought a search team in to find out why. They had worked out down to the kilowatt what each residence and business should need to live or function, respectively. No more than ten percent overage was allowed. Instead, Virgil had lined the underground walls of the once larger cold storage area with sheets of insulation everywhere except the meat area. Those walls were the original rock. A floor had been constructed of slats from broken pallets in the front section. Flat stones had been laid over the dirt in the back. A small vent at the top of the room let the cold air in from outside and was hidden by a huge planter next to the store. Plastic sheeting hanging from the ceiling kept the cold confined to the back. The cold storage was only good for the winter months, but food was easier to find in the summer. Archie helped him hang the legs. Virgil laid the tenderloins on a cutting table.

"Go ahead and help yourself to some goods, Archie. I'll get this squared away."

Archie went back out to the shelves. He pulled an old used trash bag from his pack and started placing items in it. He got some canned food, toilet paper, soap, and the staples he had mentioned. He grabbed a slightly used towel and washcloth, since the ones he had were wearing thin. A couple of pairs of thermal socks and undershirts went on top, as he closed the bag and threw it over his shoulder. Virgil came through the sheeting wiping his hands on a paper towel.

"That's a beautiful buck, Arch. I'll make sure the street folks get theirs." He looked at the bag Archie was holding. "I don't think you got enough for all that meat. You sure you don't want to grab a few more things?"

Archie shook his head. "Nah, I'm good. I don't need a lot. The coffee is the best thing I got. I haven't had any in a couple of months. Been drinking dandelion root coffee. Not the same but it does in a rush. If you think you still owe me in trade, give something to my people in the street. I'll try to stop and see some of them on my way out of town, let them know you've got something for them. See ya in a few weeks. Thanks, Virgil."

Archie started up the stairs and Virgil hurried to catch up to him. "No, thank you, Archie. The meat you bring really helps everybody. They don't get enough protein — not good quality protein anyway. That ungraded meat they send us to sell is crap. Stringy, old, just nasty looking and full of hormones and soybeans. Nobody wants it. I wouldn't eat it either. Once I put the word out I've get real meat, it'll be gone in a couple of days. Your game is always welcome here. Hell, you can bring it once a week if you want to."

"Better not. I don't want to draw any attention to you or me. About once a month is safe." Archie loaded his bag in the cart of his bike. He didn't have to worry about hiding it. The homeless all had trash bags with them carrying their most prized possessions.

Virgil pushed the door open slightly and peered out, checking to see if the coast was clear. Seeing no one, he opened the door wider so that Archie could get his bike out. Once he was clear, Archie mounted his bike, turned and waved to Virgil, then proceeded back down the alley the way he had come. Virgil watched until Archie was out of sight, took one more look around, then closed and locked the door. He headed back toward the front of his shop.

Neither of them had seen the Chinese soldier watching the entire scene from the side of the building across the alley, curiosity and suspicion written on his face. They didn't know as soon as they were out of sight he hurried off to find his superior officer. The trouble they had worked so hard to avoid all those months had found them.

7

When the front door opened, Virgil looked up from the paperwork he was trying to catch up on. A team of five Chinese soldiers came in, looking around the store. Trying to hide his concern, Virgil said, "What can I do for you gentlemen?"

The soldiers did not reply and continued to peer into every corner of the shop, working their way to the doorway that led to the back. As one of them went through, he called back to Virgil.

"What in back?" he asked in a brusque tone.

"Storage for overstock," Virgil replied without elaborating.

The soldier opened the door that led to the basement. "What down here?"

"More storage, some old shelves, that kind of thing." Virgil was getting nervous. No patrols had been in his shop since right before the invasion. That was also before he started his secondary business.

The soldier tried the door and found it locked. He

stepped back into Virgil's view and said in a menacing tone, "We inspect. You unlock door. Now!"

"Sure thing. One sec, let me get the key." Virgil's hands were shaking slightly as he reached under the counter for the key ring. He walked to the door, grasping his left hand with the right to stop the keys from jangling. The soldier stepped aside only slightly as Virgil reached the door. Steadying his hand, he stuck the key in the knob and opened it. The soldier rudely pushed him aside as he descended the staircase. The rest of his team followed. Virgil brought up the rear.

The soldiers poked their rifle barrels into shelves, spreading the contents out so they could see behind them and consequently knocking items to the floor. Virgil grimaced as a stack of canned goods toppled and a number of them hit the concrete floor. The men talked among themselves in their own language, laughing at comments Virgil couldn't understand. When they got to the shelf in the back, Virgil involuntarily held his breath. They poked and prodded the items on the shelf. Apparently satisfied there was nothing amiss, the leader of the group spoke to Virgil.

"Man seen leaving here on some kind of rickshaw bike earlier. Who is he?"

Virgil released a bit of air and replied, "Oh, he's just a homeless guy I know. I let him come in to use the bathroom."

"Name?" he said, pulling out a pad and pen.

"Uh, Virgil Chandler."

The soldier squinted his eyes at Virgil. "No, his name. I know your name. Your shop registered to sell. What is his name?"

"Oh, sorry, I misunderstood. His name is Archie."

The soldier wrote that down, paused, then looked up at Virgil. When Virgil didn't speak, he barked, "Last name!"

"Oh, uh, well, I don't know. The homeless don't like people knowing a lot about them."

The man spoke in his native tongue to one of his fellow teammates, then turned his attention back to Virgil. "Where does he live?"

Virgil shrugged and said, "Somewhere on the streets, I guess. They don't usually share where they're staying with people who aren't like them. You know ... homeless."

"What he have in bike basket?" the soldier pressed.

"I have no idea. They find stuff on the streets or in dumpsters and they keep it in bags that they have with them all the time. To us it's junk. To them, it's their prized possessions."

"How often he comes here?" the man asked as he continued his barrage of questions.

"Maybe once every month or two." Virgil tried to keep his answers short and to the point. He didn't want to slip up and say anything that might get Archie in trouble. Or more trouble, as seemed to be the case.

The spokesman looked around the room once more. With a jerk of his head and what sounded like a command, he and his men headed up the stairs. Virgil released a breath he didn't realize he was holding. The soldiers proceeded to the door where the leader stopped and turned back to Virgil.

"We'll be back. Soon. If he come back, you ask where he stays."

"Um, okay. Can I ask why you want to find him so bad?" Virgil asked.

"Nothing for you to worry about," the man said as he went to the door. He didn't say anything else.

Virgil watched through the window as the team made their way down the street. When he could no longer see them, he went back and locked the basement door again. He sat down on a chair and thought about the search.

What did they see? Why do they want to find Archie so bad? The thoughts ran through his head. He needed to find a way to get word to Archie to be careful when he came to town. But with him having no phone, Virgil had no way to get in touch with him. He stood with a sigh and headed to the counter to finish his paperwork. It was due the first of the month. He'd try to figure out how to contact his friend later.

When the door opened again, he looked up to find a Chinese man in a business suit wearing round wire-rimmed glasses. He was flanked by two soldiers. One of them turned the Open sign around to Closed and locked the door.

The man in the suit smiled and said, "Hello, Mr. Chandler. I'd like to have a word with you about your shop."

8

Archie took the long way through town in the hopes of finding some of his homeless friends. Della was picking through a garbage bin on the corner of Welsh and Poplar. He pulled up beside her.

"Hello, Darling Della," he called out as he coasted to a stop. "What are you out looking for on this cold day?"

Della looked up and smiled at him, a smile missing most of its teeth, and said, "You big flirt. I was just hoping to find another pair of socks. The ones I'm wearing have about had it." She pulled off a well-worn shoe and held up her foot. Though it was hard to distinguish behind her dirty foot and the filthy sock, he could see the entire toe section was almost gone. The shoes were castoffs of the summer slip-ons the workers wore. As she held it in her hand, he could see that she had cardboard inside it covering a hole in the bottom.

Archie reached inside the bag he had filled at Virgil's store and pulled out a brand-new pair of thermal socks. He held them out to Della. "Here, take these."

She started shaking her head. "No, Arch, I can't take your stuff. You need it just like we do."

"I insist. I have more." He pulled out the second pair he had picked up and held them for her to see. "Who needs more than a couple of pairs of socks? You only have one pair of feet to put in them."

Della hesitated, then reached out to take the proffered gift. "Thank you, Archie. You're so good to me — to all of us out here."

Grinning, he put the second pair back in his bag. "You know what they say: do good things and they will come back to you tenfold. Looks like I've got ten pairs of socks coming to me at some point."

She laughed then sat down on the curb and put the new socks on over her old ragged ones. Slipping her feet back into the shoes, she wiggled her toes and looked up at him with her big toothless smile.

"Oh, they are so warm, Archie. Thank you! Now maybe my shoes will stay on, too, since they're a bit big. You're the best!"

He patted her on the shoulder. "You know I'll always share with you if I can, Della." He looked around and down the street toward the alley where many of the homeless spent their time. "Say, where is everybody? I figured this place would be a lot more crowded."

Della leaned in conspiratorially and whispered, "They're taking everybody, Archie. Every day a few more disappear. No one wants to be caught by a patrol. If I didn't need the socks so bad, you likely wouldn't have found me either."

"Taking them where?" he asked, concern apparent in his tone.

Della shook her head. "No one knows because none of them ever comes back. I heard some of those Russian guys talking the other day, and they said something about the Chinese cleaning up the trash on the streets. I thought they were talking about garbage. Now I know they were talking about us."

Archie frowned as he mulled over what Della had told him. If what she said was true, then it wouldn't be safe for him in town anymore. And it wasn't safe for Della now.

"Della, come out to the farm with me. It's dangerous for you here. I have a good setup out there with plenty of room, so you can have your privacy, but you won't be alone. Please."

Della looked down then back up into Archie's eyes. Tears were forming that she didn't try to hide. With a sad smile she said, "I can't. This is my home. This is where I belong."

Anger rose in his face. Gritting his teeth to keep from shouting, he replied, "What happens when they find you? They will, you know. It sounds like they won't rest until everyone who lives on the streets is dead!"

Still smiling, Della said quietly, "If the good Lord is ready for me, I'm ready to go. Now, you better get moving, Arch, before a patrol comes by and catches you. Give us a hug and get going."

She held her arms out to him. He leaned in and squeezed her tight. "Stay hid, Darling Della. I want to see you the next time I come to town."

She leaned back and looked into his eyes again. "I'd like that, honey. Love you."

"Love you, too." Archie watched as she shuffled off toward the alley with her dilapidated shopping cart. He knew she wouldn't hide. He was pretty sure he'd never see her again. Sadly, he turned his bike around to head back home.

He had gone about a block when the patrol car pulled up in front of him.

9

ARCHIE CAME to a stop in front of the car. It was really an SUV and all four doors opened as six soldiers quickly exited the vehicle. They brought their rifles to bear on Archie who slowly raised his hands.

In a calm voice, Archie said, "Is there a problem, fellas?"

"Get off bike!" one of the soldiers shouted. "Down on ground!" The team of soldiers advanced as Archie stepped off his bike and knelt beside it.

"What's going on? Did I do something wrong?" Archie asked in a tension-laced voice. He knew if they searched his basket there would be trouble. A homeless person shouldn't have the things he had traded for the deer meat.

"Name!" the soldier shouted.

"Archie." When the soldier continued to glare at him, he added, "Hogan."

"Why you out in day? Why you not working?"

Archie replied, "I'm a disabled vet. I can't stand on my feet all day. I decided to just live off the land on my own."

The speaker advanced on him. "Where you live? I not see your bike in city."

"No, I live out in the country." He didn't elaborate.

"*Where?*" the soldier yelled as he leaned down into Archie's face.

Archie flinched at the sudden tone change and pulled back away from the man. "It's about five miles from here up Highway 9. An old abandoned farm."

With a satisfied smirk, the man replied, "Aha! You trespass!"

"It's abandoned! No one lives there!"

The soldier crossed his arms. "Any property that owner not live on anymore belongs to government. You trespass."

While this exchange was going on, two of the other men had been removing the items from the basket of Archie's bike. When they got to the black garbage bag, one of them called out to his team leader. Archie turned toward the new voice, saw what was happening, and closed his eyes. It was over.

The leader went over and looked inside the bag. His eyes grew wide. He ran the few steps to where Archie still knelt, his left knee throbbing so badly he wanted to cry out in pain. The soldier grabbed him by his coat and drug him to his own bike.

"Where you get this? You no have credits if you no work! You steal this!" He waved a hand toward the basket.

Archie shook his head. Defeated, he replied, "I traded for it."

"Who? Who you trade with? What you trade for it? Where you trade?"

He didn't know they had seen him leaving Virgil's shop, but he fabricated a story anyway. "I find stuff in old empty houses. I trade it for other stuff. I trade with lots of people all over the place. I don't know their names or where they live. We just find each other."

"You trespass and steal! You prisoner now!" He turned to

his men and spoke to them in their native tongue. One of them got on his radio and called something in. Another one turned Archie around roughly and handcuffed him. The bag of goods was taken and put in the back of the SUV.

A real patrol car, formerly used by the city police, pulled up. Another Chinese man got out and shoved Archie roughly into the back seat. As he slammed the door, Archie watched out the window as his precious bike was beaten with batons until it was hardly recognizable. Once they had rendered it useless, they tossed it into the back of the SUV.

Archie didn't know where they were taking him. He did know one thing though — it was the last place he would ever see.

10

The patrol car headed out of town in the opposite direction of Archie's place. Archie hadn't been out that way in quite a while, since before the invasion. It wouldn't have mattered. It didn't look anything like it did back then. It looked more like a garrison post — or a concentration camp. Razor wire topped a ten-foot high fence surrounding the area. The car pulled through the gate when it was opened and parked in front of what looked like some sort of administration building. Archie was looking the place over and saw a number of barracks-style housing units. The people milling around looked lost. They wore clothes exactly like the ones worn by the workers in town, with the exception of the color. These were bright orange.

"What is this place?" Archie asked the question aloud though he hadn't meant to. The "policeman" who had driven there turned to glare at him.

"No talking!"

Archie didn't have to wait long to get his answer though. A soldier walked over and pulled the door open, then grabbed Archie's arm and pulled him roughly from the back seat. In the process, Archie's foot caught under the seat in front of him and the force being applied to his arm caused his bad knee to be twisted painfully. He yelped involuntarily at the same time he heard the knee pop.

"Stop! Wait a minute!" he yelled as the soldier continued to drag him from the vehicle, either not realizing his prisoner was in agony or, more likely, not caring. He dropped Archie unceremoniously on the ground then prodded him sharply with the muzzle of his weapon.

"Stand up!"

In a half-fetal position, Archie looked up at the soldier with tears streaming down his face. "I can't," he replied in a pain-laced voice "My knee is messed up."

"Stand!" the man yelled at him again, this time poking him sharply with his rifle.

Angered by the assault, Archie rolled over to try to rise. There was no way to do it with hands secured behind him. He only had one good knee, and it wasn't enough to get him up. The soldier standing over him was joined by the two men who had escorted Archie to the camp. They all stood watching and snickering as he tried to stand. None of them offered to help.

Archie tried but wasn't able to comply. Finally, the driver and his partner went over and pulled Archie roughly to his feet. Standing as tall as he could, he glared at the men.

"Glad you enjoyed the show. Now what?"

The driver, who still had a hand on Archie's arm, turned him, backhanding Archie across the face. "I said no talking!"

Archie's head snapped toward his right shoulder with the blow. Tasting the coppery flavor of his own blood, he turned his head slowly back to the Chinese men and stared menacingly at them as he slipped his tongue out to the side of his injured mouth. He stood silently waiting for them to continue.

The one who had jabbed him with his rifle grabbed his arm to pull him along. When his own weight hit Archie's bad knee, it buckled, but he stayed upright. He was guided to the building just ahead. When they reached the door, the driver opened it and shoved Archie inside. The men didn't enter. The door was closed behind him. He stood staring into the dark room waiting for his eyes to adjust after being out in the bright sun. Once his eyes had adjusted, he saw a table with a chair on one side. A Chinese man in a business suit was sitting in it. Light from a single window cast the man in a soft glow. He was writing something on the paper in front of him. After a moment, he looked up.

"Come forward, Mr. Hogan." His voice was calm and his English impeccable. Archie limped over to the table. The man saw his distress. "You are injured. Are you in need of medical assistance?"

Someone had obviously radioed ahead and given him Archie's name and God knew what else. Archie shook his head. "Nah, I'm good." He shifted his weight to his good leg and stared at the man. The man returned his gaze.

Taking his round-rimmed glasses off and pulling a handkerchief out of his coat pocket, the man started cleaning his glasses. He looked up at Archie and replied in a calm even tone, "Very well then. My name is Doctor Huang. I am a procurer of information for the Chinese Republic. You were found with a number of items that a person who does not work in the factories should not be able to buy. Where did you get them?"

Archie considered his answer. He would never name Virgil, so he kept it vague. "I traded for them."

"Who did you trade with?"

Archie shrugged. "Different people. I've got a lot of friends in town still."

"Names?" Doctor Huang continued to clean his glasses,

seeming engrossed in the action, as he wasn't looking at Archie.

"I'd rather not say. What difference does it make?"

Ignoring Archie's question, Huang went on. "And what did you trade? What did you have that would be of value to someone else?"

"I find things everywhere. People throw good stuff away all the time. One man's trash is another man's treasure. That's a saying we have in this country."

Huang put his glasses back on and finally looked at Archie. "But the things in your basket were new. There was nothing there someone might have thrown out."

"I'd finished my trading for the day. I found takers for all the stuff I had. It was a good day ... until your men grabbed me."

Leaning forward, Huang pierced Archie with a steely gaze. "So, this is the story you are going to stick with then?"

Archie hesitated. Something wasn't right. The man was too smug. There was something he knew that Archie didn't. Still, he couldn't change directions. "It's the truth. Why wouldn't I stick with it?"

Huang stood and with a wicked sneer called out, "Bring him in!"

The door opened drawing Archie's attention. Two soldiers came into the room dragging another man who appeared to be unconscious. They dropped him unceremoniously on the floor at Archie's feet. With a moan laced in pain, the man turned to his side. It was Virgil. Archie's eyes grew wide. His friend had been beaten to a bloody pulp, his face barely recognizable. One of his arms was dislocated at the shoulder and hung at an awkward angle from his body. His feet were bare, and Archie could tell they were severely broken, as if someone had taken a metal pipe and hit them multiple times.

With his hands still cuffed, Archie couldn't reach out to him, but he dropped to his knees, ignoring the pain, and leaned over him. "Virgil! Virgil! Can you hear me? It's Archie!"

Virgil turned his face fully in Archie's direction. Both eyes were swollen shut, his nose and jaw obviously broken. After a few seconds, he mumbled, "I'm sorry, Arch."

Archie could barely make out what he'd said. "For what? You have nothing to be sorry for, my friend." He pulled his gaze away from his broken buddy and glared viciously at Huang. "Why? Why did you do this?"

"Because we do not condone practices outside of what we have dictated as the proper ways to conduct business. Mr. Chandler was found to have another business on his premises that was not approved by the government. But you knew that already, didn't you, Mr. Hogan?"

Archie pressed his lips together not bothering to answer the question. Huang went on.

"You were seen leaving the rear of Mr. Chandler's shop earlier today. It is a relatively good conclusion that anyone leaving by the back is doing something he does not want others to know about. We performed a most thorough search of his shop and found the secret room. So, tell me — what did you use to kill the deer? You know that weapons are not allowed to be owned by anyone but our police or military. I'm sure you didn't chase it down. Where is the weapon?"

Archie was seething in rage. "You all but killed this man over a *deer*? What the hell is wrong with you people? Having deer meat isn't against any of your laws!"

"He chose not to reveal the person who had brought him the deer. Well, he tried at first." Huang pointed at Virgil's broken body lying on the floor. "After more intense interrogation, he decided it would be prudent to give us the information we wanted. His secret room, his way of procuring supplies ... and the person who brought the meat."

"Well, maybe if the meat you offered the people to eat was actually *edible*, they wouldn't *need* to find it from other places!" Archie's rage was growing. He didn't care what the consequences were. "That pasty tripe you call meat at the grocery store is as likely to make someone sick as anything. I can't imagine it has any nutritional value. Meat is supposed to be red, not white!"

At the sound of his raised voice, the soldiers started toward Archie, but Huang held up a hand. The soldiers stopped their advance but stayed where they were, just behind Archie.

"You may not be aware, Mr. Hogan, but the meat we provide to the citizens is safe and nutritious. It is treated with many vitamins and nutrients to fulfill the dietary needs of the workers."

"Yeah, I'm aware. I'm also aware that you suck the blood out of it, so you can transport it from here to China and back here again without it going rancid. It's disgusting, and I don't blame anybody for not wanting to eat it!"

"Thank you for sharing your insight into our food production process. Now, back to my question. What did you use to kill the deer?"

"A bow and arrows I made myself. Just for hunting — real meat."

Huang nodded. "You made this weapon knowing it was illegal, correct?"

"I made it so I could eat. You people made it illegal. Bows and arrows have been used in this country for thousands of years."

Huang stood up and walked around the table to where Archie was kneeling beside Virgil. Leaning down into his face, he leered at Archie with an evil smile. "Thank you for your confession, Mr. Hogan. The sentence is death. Take them both outside. That one has bled on my floor long enough."

The soldiers each grabbed one of Virgil's arms and the one closest grabbed Archie by the cuffs and yanked him up. They dragged both men out into the yard and dropped them. Doctor Huang followed with a megaphone.

"Attention! Everyone to the yard at once!" His voice brought the people in the yard out of their stupors as they hurried to obey his command. They clustered together, keeping their distance from the soldiers and the two men lying on the ground. When they were all gathered around, Huang spoke into the megaphone again.

"These two men have broken numerous laws. Their sentence is death. You shall all witness it and know that while we are generous to those who obey the rules, justice is swift for those who do not. Do you have any last words, Mr. Hogan?"

Archie looked at the frightened faces staring back at him. These people who, less than a year ago, lived normal lives — working, playing with their kids, going out on dates, ordering pizza, and watching a movie at home — had become lifeless, hollow-eyed beings, existing in someone else's universe; their zest for life drained as they worked mundane jobs for sustenance. Their dreams had been shattered because an out-of-control government spent money it didn't have on their behalf and couldn't pay back when the call was made. He felt he needed to try something, anything, to awaken even one of them from the trance-like lives they were living.

"You all need to wake up! You're letting them steal your lives! Find a reason to live!" Archie heard the charging handle being pulled back on the rifle behind him, loading the round that would end his existence. As he felt the steel touch the back of his head he shouted, "I die free!"

The teenage boy was scouring the ground where he had watched them destroy the homeless man's bike. A glint from the sun caught his eye. Reaching down, he picked up a medal — a Purple Heart. He pinned it inside his coat. He caught up with his friends and they continued toward the edge of town.

"Let's go find the militia and get our country back, guys."

PART II: A.R.C.H.I.E.

Written by L. Douglas Hogan

11

SIX WEEKS after Archie's death

After Archie was executed on the cold winter streets, word began to spread of his murder. Within weeks, counter-offensive groups were secretly gathering in the dark recesses of the city as underground networks of communication began to develop and become more sophisticated. It wasn't safe to meet in public anymore. Any open gathering of two or more people drew heavy suspicions. The Chinese were particularly weary of American resourcefulness and resolve. The invaders were a studious group that were well-educated on American history and their spirit of independence. When they were trained, they were taught to never underestimate the tiniest detail, for in them could be found American strength.

The organized Armed Services as Americans knew it was long gone. Betrayed by their very own government, most of them went AWOL while others splintered away. Nobody knew how to contact them or even where they were located. Some of them remained behind and assisted with the fight for liberty. At least for now, the surviving Americans were on their own, separated from the larger, more organized and armed military groups. Beneath the city streets, patriots were meeting to discuss plans on developing an effective counterinsurgency. Small bands of survivors, that never left the cityscape, began to rally. They worked secretly and tirelessly on their methods of recruitment, knowing full well that they would not outlast the well-equipped Chinese military without an army of their own. The small groups of militias each had a veteran in charge as the commander.

"What sense does it make to sit around and just let them run things? This is our country. Men like Archie gave their lives in defense of our freedom," the young adult male said. He spoke with passion as he attempted to make a prevailing point to attack the Chinese now, while they were off-guard.

"Keep your voice down, David!" the leader of the command said. "These tunnels carry sound far and wide. If the Chins hear us, there'll be nowhere left for us to hide."

David held his tongue, but he did so with indignation. He was ambitious and gung-ho. David was one of six teenage boys they were using to spy on the Chinese. American militias used them because they were less conspicuous. Their small frames and dexterity, along with their non-threatening size, made them the perfect intelligence gatherers. The group's leader, Kyle Vanhorn, was one of thousands of servicemen deserters that disappeared when the government allowed the Chinese to take over. He appreciated the teenager's assistance and opinions, but the boy was far too immature to assist in coordinating sophisticated attacks on the invaders. He knew David's point was valid, but kids had little understanding of the importance of patience. It would take time to coordinate an effective attack with minimal casualties. When he saw David was calm, he continued his speech. "We need to let the Chins believe they have things all wrapped up. I've heard of other survivors and ongoing combat in the southern states. Just last night, the Chins sent a battalion-sized unit to Texas to help bring the fight to an end. If we can keep things hot here, it may give the South a fighting chance, but as long as they keep sending reinforcements, they're screwed."

"So, the plan is to draw more attention to us, so our fight gets harder?" David said with a confrontational tone.

"David, there's not going to be a fight anywhere if we all can't pull our own weight. If every commander for every militia does what I'm about to say, then we can both draw down their numbers and cause confusion among the Chinese ranks." Kyle didn't like arguing with a teenager, but the group desperately needed his services. For now, it appeared as if David might have spoken his peace. Kyle looked up at the other commanders; each of them seemed amused that he was arguing with a kid. Kyle hoped that three of them could empathize with the situation.

"What do you have for us?" the commander of a neighboring militia asked, breaking the awkward silence. Kyle was glad for it.

"The Chinese executed a Purple Heart recipient not long ago. The man's name was Archie. He was a well-liked veteran that gave of himself his entire life. Even as a homeless veteran, he gave. He never quit giving. So, I came up with a counterinsurgency plan to honor Archie. It's an acronym that we can all commit to memory. We'll remember it because it spells out his name." Kyle could see the faces of the militia members as they focused in anticipation on his next words. David was especially happy because he saw what they did to Archie. He heard Archie's final words. He couldn't shake them. Kyle continued.

"As you know, suburban warfare is considerably dangerous. A head-on assault by largely unskilled men and women would be suicide. That's why we have to use both guerilla and traditional tactics. Each of us have skills we can bring to the table. David, Kaleb, Joey, Scottie, Squish, and Tyler, our Teen Team, are smaller and less suspicious looking. They bring the element of surprise to the group. Commanders bring their military training and leadership to the group. Each group has members that are experts in something. If you know what your group's strengths are, then bring them here tomorrow. If you don't know, find out what they are and bring them back.

"This acronym will be the most effective if we can assign specific tasks to the right people. Once we know who can do what, we can capitalize on that. The first letter in the acronym is A for *ambush*. We will coordinate our attack by studying our enemy. After the attack, we move to the second letter of the acronym, R. R stands for *retreat*. Don't worry, David. It's only a temporary move that sets us up for the next. The C stands for *convalesce*. After we retreat, we break up and gather our bearings. Whatever you do, do not retreat as a group. Fall back to positions that offer you the best safety. We're too small of a group to move together. If they catch even a small group, it'll be a wash.

That same night make your way back here. This is where we'll regroup and *hide*, which is the fourth letter of the acronym. We'll stay hidden until we can go over the *intelligence* that each of us collects from the ambush. After the intelligence has been shared, we'll use it to *enlist* new members to the cause. Knowledge is power, but we'll have no strength without the numbers.

"That's it. Ambush, Retreat, Convalesce, Hide, share Intelligence, and Enlist new members. We can do this if we do it smart. What do you guys think?"

They all looked around the dimly lit room at one another. They were sold. It was easy to tell. Most of them had half-smiles.

"I like it," Commander Trish Glaspy said. She was a

sergeant in the Army before the invasion. A single mother of two until the Chinese arrived. After that, the kids were taken and moved elsewhere. Rumor on the street was that they were being indoctrinated with communist propaganda. There was really no reason to believe anything else. Making homeless people disappear was easy to cover up, but not children. The global community would investigate. That would cause more problems than the Chinese government was willing to deal with. "I like it a lot," she said with several head nods.

"Me too," Commander Joseph Lyautey said. "You can count on my group."

Vanhorn, Glaspy, and Lyautey were looking at Commander Trenton Beck and waiting for a response. "It's too risky," he said, breaking the unity of the alliance.

"Too risky, how?" Lyautey asked. "What do we need to spell out to get you on board?"

"Their numbers are too great and we're too small. I can't see a viable way of fighting back without losing numbers. Eventually the Chinese will catch on and they'll hammer us. There'll be a swift and heavy-handed retribution."

Kyle shrugged his shoulders and squinted his eyes in disbelief at Beck's response. "What's the point of having numbers if you're not going to use them to fight? We can't continue to let them intimidate with threats and control us with food and water. Think of it this way, each ambush ends with enlisting more numbers. Numbers are a good thing! When people see we're fighting back, they will be encouraged to do the same. If we can't defeat them outright, then this is what we have to do."

"Fine, I'm agreeing under duress, but if things go south, I'm going to do what I have to do to protect my group. To protect my family!" Beck said. The answer was less than desirable for the others, but they didn't want to press him on an issue he was already wavering on. There was a tinge of mistrust, but it'd have to do.

"Okay, then," Kyle said. "Let's meet back here tomorrow at this time. We'll go over our assets and liabilities. After that, we'll spend a week gathering intel on Chinese movement. We have to take this nice and slow. We can't make unprepped moves," he said, looking specifically at David.

"We have to be smart and patient. David, take your crew topside and spend the next week acting normal. Do not write things down! Commit them to your memory and share them with each other. If you're caught and searched and they find proof of insurrection, they'll execute you publicly, on the spot, just like they did Archie. Stay alive. The memory of six is better than one. We need to know the who, what, when, where, and how of everything you take a mental note of. If there's too much to remember, bring your intel back, but never do anything in a routine. Use different trails. Take different manholes to get here, leave at different times. Keep moving. A moving target is harder to acquire. Stay fluid and allow for change of plan."

Kyle extended his hand to David. David reached into his coat and pulled something out and held it in the fist of his right hand.

"Fifty thousand of these have been issued since the Gulf War. They all carry significance, but this one's special," David said, speaking somewhat inexplicably.

After shaking Kyle's hand, he turned and walked away with his group of teenage friends. Kyle opened his hand to see what David left behind from his handshake. His words now made sense. It was Archie's Purple Heart medal. Kyle stood in silence and disbelief, staring into his own hand. When he finally looked up, David was standing at the corner of one of the tunnels. He nodded to Kyle, then turned and walked out.

12

THE NEXT MORNING, Kyle was fast asleep when a sudden heavy pounding sound came from the front door. Both he and his wife were startled awake by the event. Surprised that somebody was at his door, he shot up out of the bed and threw on a pair of pants.

"Faith, you have two minutes to get Kayla to her hiding spot. Go on, now — just as we rehearsed," he said, fastening his belt. Kyle's wife, Faith, jumped out of the bed and darted for their daughter Kayla's room. She didn't even bother to clothe herself. In a flash, she was out of Kyle's sight and he was walking for the front door.

They had rehearsed this eventuality a hundred times over. He knew it would come, he just didn't know when. It was no secret that every child in the inner city was disappearing. The rumor was that they were being whisked away for the purpose of indoctrinating the next generation of Americans; ensuring the future of Chinese control over America meant having a communist country sympathetic to Chinese rule. China always thought long-term. They understood, all too well, that the defeat and financial fall of the American way of life would have to be a waiting game – a game of patience. Defeating America without ever pulling the trigger was the goal.

Kyle didn't want to keep his company waiting. He knew that from a strategic standpoint, making the people at the door wait would arouse suspicion. The goal, Kyle taught his wife and daughter, was to appear normal, non-threatening, and cooperative. A timely response alleviates suspicions.

Keep calm and cooperative, Kyle thought. He opened the front room door. Just as he suspected, there were three Chinese soldiers standing on his porch. One had a rifle in hand, the second had a rifle on his shoulder, and the third had a pistol on his hip and a clipboard in his hands.

"Good morning," Kyle said, wiping the sleep from his eyes.

The soldiers inspected his appearance. It was clear that he was just out of bed. Sleep marks lined his face and his hair was shoved to one side.

"Mr. Vanhorn?" the Chinese man with the clipboard asked.

"Yes, how can I help you?"

The other two Chinese men pushed past Kyle and entered his home. Kyle wanted to stop them, but he knew doing so would get him shot. He let them pass. "What's this about?" he asked the last man, just as his wife was rejoining him in the living room.

"You on suspect list," the man answered. He was obviously English-speaking, just bad at it.

"Suspect list? What suspect list?"

The man ignored Kyle's question by asking one of his own. "How many in family?"

"Just me and my wife, Faith. What's this about?"

"You have guns?"

"No. I would never do anything to violate the law or the

rules of the CTS." The CTS was the modified Communist Totalitarian Society. The group governed the workforce but was expanding to include security services and other military-related projects.

"The Motherland say you have guns."

"I used to have guns, but I –"

The Chinese man interrupted Kyle. "...and a child. Where child?"

"My child disappeared. I thought you took her," Kyle answered with indignation. Kyle had to act angry over the lie he was trying to sell the Chinaman. Any good lie had to be compelling if it was going to be believed.

"You not know where your child is. You bad parent."

Kyle didn't answer. The two men that pushed past Kyle were already ransacking the house. They went into the front room taking photos out of the frames and letting them fall to the floor. "C'mon!" Kyle yelled. "You're not going to find guns in picture frames."

"You have guns then?" the nicely dressed Chinese man asked.

"No. I'm just saying that what they're looking for won't fit into the places they're searching." Nothing was being returned to its place. The men moved to the kitchen, destroying everything as they went.

"When last time you see daughter?"

The particulars of the question weren't rehearsed by Kyle. The answer depended solely upon the timeframe in which the Chinese began moving the children into custodial care. The answer was an unknown. "I don't remember. It's been a while."

One of the Chinese men that were in the kitchen said something in Mandarin. "Xiānshēng. Pánzi."

Kyle turned around and looked through the corridor that

led to the kitchen. He had no idea what he was saying. The man at the sink was holding up three plastic cups.

"Why three cups?" the Chinese man asked.

"Because I drank water before we ate supper last night."

The man at the sink pulled three dishes out of the sink.

"You do everything three time?" The man asked.

"Am I not allowed to eat off of my own dishes whenever I want?"

Faith made her way to the bedroom and put some clothes on after she successfully hid Kayla. After that, she rejoined Kyle in the front room. She was worried about the Chinese men's search of their home and beginning to get antsy.

The third intruder came out from the back room. He was holding a pair of dirty socks that appeared to belong to a smaller person. A child, perhaps. Kayla was ten years old. Kyle knew the communist mindset enough to know that he was on borrowed time now. His every answer was going to be insufficient and the intruders were invasive enough that he knew they would eventually find his daughter. He couldn't let that happen.

The Chinese man that was in the kitchen walked over to the other one with socks in hand and spoke to him in Mandarin. Then they both walked off to the back of the house where Kayla was hiding. This could be Kyle's only window of opportunity to save his family. He reached over for the bookshelf and grabbed a heavy marble statue. He used it to smash the well-dressed man in the head. The man instantly collapsed. Faith looked up to Kyle for guidance. He pulled his finger up to his lips, signaling her to remain silent.

This is it. No turning back now. Kyle knew that if he were to get caught, the punishment would be extreme. He, his wife, his daughter, possibly even his friends, would all be publicly executed. Just under the window, the fish tank harbored a dark secret. He reached in and burrowed his fingers beneath the aquarium rock and pulled out a vacuum-sealed bag. Its contents? A fully loaded Smith & Wesson 38 Special. Its small frame made it perfect for concealing in tight spaces. The vacuum-sealed bag had a tear-away tab that he used to open it.

Time was of the essence. At any moment, the other two armed Chinese military men might walk out of the back room and see what he had done. The way Kyle saw it, he had two choices. Hide the body in the closet or immediately engage the other two. He chose the latter. They were moments from finding Kayla, so the time to act was now. Faith wasn't a weak woman, but there was only one gun hidden in the house. The best thing for her to do at the moment was to stay out of the way and let Kyle do his thing.

The men were in Kayla's room ransacking everything. They were cutting open her stuffed animals and pulling the stuffing out onto the floor, gutting the mattresses and pillows, pulling drawers out of the dresser, and doing whatever they could to show their authority and control over the residence.

Kyle entered the hallway where Kayla's room was attached and peered down the hall. Both men were in her room. Kayla may be safe for the time being, but it was only a matter of time until she was discovered. He quietly snuck down the hallway until he came to her room. With pistol in hand, he brought it up and spun around to face the entrance, not knowing what he was going to face. Luckily, both men were preoccupied destroying Kayla's room. He brought his S&W up and pointed it at the back of the closest man's head. He pulled the trigger and a loud *kaboom* was heard throughout the neighborhood. The man's head swallowed the 158-grain projectile. The man dropped limp to the floor.

The other man turned around to face his comrade's killer, but he was too late. Kyle pulled the trigger a second time. The bullet hit the man just under the left eye. The sudden pressure popped the Chinese man's eyeball from its socket, but it mattered little. He would no longer have a use for it. The second man died on Kayla's hiding spot beneath the floor. Kyle dragged his body out of the way then pulled the rug up, revealing a hiding space beneath the planks of the floorboards. He did the secret knock that they rehearsed, and Kayla lifted the hatch and peeked out.

"It's safe, baby, but we need to leave now," her daddy explained.

Faith came running in after the sound of the second gun shot. She was standing in the doorway of Kayla's room as Kyle was pulling her out of the floor. He looked up at Faith and asked, "Can you take Kayla to the kitchen? Keep her occupied for two or three minutes."

Faith acknowledged him then took Kayla by the hand and led her to the kitchen area, saying, "Keep your eyes closed, honey."

Kyle dragged the two men into position over Kayla's old hiding spot and pushed them into it. The spot was made by Kyle to hide him, Faith, and Kayla, so he knew it would work as a hiding place for his intruders. When the two men were in place, he headed to the front room and hoisted the leader of the trio onto his shoulders. He carried him to Kayla's room and dumped him on top of the other two. Once they were all hidden, he replaced the wooden hatch and rug. His work wasn't quite done. There was some blood on the wooden floor that needed to be cleaned up. Some soap and bleach from under the kitchen sink would do the job. It wouldn't hide the evidence from a forensic team, but it would work against an inspection for missing Chinese soldiers and government officials.

When the work was done, the realization that they had to move Kayla to safety in broad daylight hit him like a ton of bricks.

The sound of another knock came to the back door. Kyle was carrying a five-shot and had already used two. With just three rounds left, Kyle had to be careful not to get into a firefight. With his gun hand behind his back, he looked through the window of the back door. It was his neighbor, Joe. Joe was a busybody and one that Kyle couldn't rely on to keep secrets. If he heard the gunshots, it wouldn't be long before the CTS returned.

"What's up, Joe?"

"I thought I heard gunshots," the man said.

"That's funny. I didn't hear anything," Kyle answered.

"How could you not? It was loud."

"Maybe check your other neighbor?"

"Do you have company, Mr. Vanhorn?"

"No, why do you ask?"

"I couldn't help but notice the CTS vehicles parked in front of your house."

"I'll check it out. Maybe their doing a door-to-door or something. Have a good day."

Kyle shut the door and didn't give another moment of his time to Joe.

13

Two weeks later, Kyle's original intentions were to hide the bodies and watch from a distance for a short time until he believed it would be safe to return home. The complication he didn't anticipate was Joe's interference. The keys to the CTS vehicles parked to the front of his home were on the bodies of the dead men in his daughter's floor. He would have moved the vehicles, but that would also draw suspicion. The whole visit was rehearsed, but unplanned. There's that element in every situation that calls for a bit of ad-lib. Unfortunately, the improvisation required too great a risk. Nothing was more important to Kyle than his family. He would give his life for them and their freedom.

A squad of Chinese soldiers occupied the block where Kyle killed the three Chinese government employees. Their bodies were discovered when Kyle's neighbor Joe reported that there were two vehicles belonging to the CTS parked in front of his neighbor's residence and that they'd been there since the day he heard two gunshots. Instead of rewarding Joe for volunteering the information to the CTS, he was publicly hanged from the tree in his yard for not disclosing to them the gunshot sounds he heard two weeks prior. They may have judged Joe for his lack of action, but before he died, he revealed everything he knew about Kyle and his family, to include his daughter. What they didn't know was, where did they go?

Kyle had a contingency plan for everything. After Joe's snoop into the Vanhorn's affairs, Kyle moved Faith and Kayla to his father-in-law's old homestead, far from the city. The house was long abandoned and was absent of electricity. It did have a handpump water well, which could supply life-giving water for as long as they needed. Food was the issue. The winter was unforgiving for plant life. The garden was long overgrown. He assured them it would only be for a short time until the current situation blew over. He promised to check back in with them frequently, then he left.

David, Kaleb, Joey, Scottie, Squish, and Tyler were riding their bikes around town and keeping an eye on the situation at the Vanhorn residence. Seeing how the entire block was under military control, they were careful to maintain their distance. They reported everything they were seeing back to Kyle at every militia meeting.

Since the introduction of A.R.C.H.I.E., several dozen enlistees were added to the cause. Resistance to the Chinese invasion was drawing more attention than they were anticipating. On a regular basis, the Chinese were having to reroute their supply paths to more viable ones. It seemed that no matter what they did, they were being hit with improvised explosive devices or their own weapons were being used against them. No American bothered walking out onto the street. Everybody knew the resistance movement against the Chinese was a dangerous one. If one wasn't fighting, they were hiding in their homes or relaying information. It seemed that the public executions had no affect on the Americans. No matter what method the Chinese used to attempt to bring about complete subjugation, it always seemed to have the opposite effect. It was time to try something new. Something radical.

That night, mobile communications units were driving up and down the city streets. It was the first time they'd been seen. Nobody attacked them for curiosity of wanting to know what they were being used for. Large sound systems were attached to the top of each unit and they played a prerecorded message from the CTS. Their purpose suddenly became clear.

"This is the Communist Totalitarian Society. We know that many of you are harboring enemies of the People's Republic of China. Effective immediately, food vouchers for the working class will be suspended pending cooperation from every able-bodied American. Your children depend on your cooperation. Additionally, if you turn in any conspirators, or provide information that leads to the arrest of conspirators, you and your family will be rewarded with double vouchers. Do not let your children down. The CTS is your friend. Cooperate with us and you will be rewarded."

It was a threat. Plain and simple. The new response from the CTS was a veiled threat to harm the children if they were met with any further resistance. The matter called for a special counterinsurgency meeting.

Later that night, below the city streets, the lights flickered eerily. The dank-smelling and moist air certainly hadn't improved. The sewers were still the best option for a meeting place. Commanders Vanhorn, Glaspy, and Lyautey were on time; however, Commander Beck was thirty minutes late. It wasn't like him to be late, so the others were beginning to act nervously.

"I don't like it," Glaspy said. "Something's off."

"I agree. Something's not right," Lyautey added.

As if on cue, the lights went out. Everybody remained quiet and waited. The power outage was followed by the sounds of manhole covers being moved. At first, they thought it might be Beck using a different access point. But then there was a second manhole cover opening. It was a dead giveaway. They had been discovered.

Flashbangs were dropped down into the tunnels. The nearest manhole was several yards away in any direction, so the blinding lights did not affect them, however the percussion of the grenades was carried throughout the tunnel system. They were deafening.

"Evacuate," Kyle said calmly, ears ringing. He didn't have to yell it. He maintained his composure and the leaders began their evacuation, even without hearing his voice. They had all been affected by the percussion and knew it was time to flee.

The Chinese made their breach. The Americans scattered in the darkness using their hands and feet to feel their way through the unlit tunnels. Beaming lights and lasers of the well-equipped invaders pierced the smoky haze. They clearly had the upper hand where rifle accessories were concerned, but the American freedom fighters knew the tunnels better.

Kyle, like the others, was making a run for it. To live to fight another day was the goal. Unlike the Chinese, the commanders and the handful of men they had with them, weren't an army equipped to handle such a force. With every turn of a tunnel, Kyle would stop just around the bend and wait for a rifle light to come around into his line of sight. He would aim down his rifle sights and take a shot a little high and to the left of the light. By his calculations, that placed each round center mass. It was a technique that seemed to be working. Each pull of the trigger dropped another invader.

What his enemy didn't know was that the tunnels were rigged to blow for such an occasion. The evacuation had been practiced a hundred times over and it was Kyle's job to make it to the detonator if they were discovered. Detonating cord was strung all along the electrical conduit that lined the upper-portions of the walls of the tunnels. At the end was the detonator and all he needed to do was prime it and ignite the charges.

"Where's that ladder?" he said aloud as he walked along toward his destination. The only thing giving him visibility was the enemy's tactical lights and he was busy shooting at them. It wasn't long before he reached his goal. "There you are, baby! Come to daddy," he said, picking up the detonator.

He primed the charge and then ignited the plastic explosives. A thunderous explosion began to erupt throughout the underground passages. The sound was deafening and left him with a ringing noise that blocked out just about everything else. He lifted the manhole cover that made his escape possible.

As he stepped up onto the ground and looked out over the city, the roadways were littered with Chinese military personnel and vehicles. The roads collapsed, sucking many of them down into the concrete and asphalt debris field. Most didn't make it. They fell in and died under tons of concrete. Nobody noticed him. He was like a ghost as they dispersed in all directions to save their own lives. The resistance had a special rendezvous point for such an event. Kyle was hopeful that the others made it out alive.

Only time would tell.

14

THE EVACUATION of the patriot resistance went without a hitch. To the credit of the resisters, twenty Chinese soldiers died in the explosion and collapsed city streets. Word of the incident traveled far and fast, even at midnight; it was less than optimal news for the Communist Totalitarian Society, but a major victory for the Americans. A swift and drastic response was to be made by the occupying forces if they were going to tighten their already loose grasp over the American populace.

A knock on the front door had a nervous Trenton Beck stand up from his sofa where he was trying to console his wife. He wanted to believe he didn't know who was knocking at his door, but he knew exactly who it was. Turning to look at his wife as he went for the door, she could tell he was afraid.

"Go hide in the basement," he said. "Just like we rehearsed. Don't come out unless I come for you."

Beck's wife ran for the basement. Once she was out of sight, he opened the door. Three Chinese soldiers stood on his doorstep. They were armed. Behind them, parked at the curb in front of his home, sat a military vehicle and a patrol car, formerly used by the municipal police.

"You Mr. Beck?" one of the men asked.

"Yes."

"You come with us, now."

Two of the three men grabbed Beck by the arms. Fearing for his wife's safety, he didn't resist. They pulled him out of his house and escorted him to the police cruiser, where the driver met them and opened the back door. They pushed Beck into the cage and closed the door. Beck inspected the environment. This was the first time he had ever sat in the back of a police car. There were no buttons or levers; nothing to operate the windows or any way to unlock and open the door. He was a prisoner. One of the two escorts stayed back with the driver, while the other two returned to the house.

"No!" Beck shouted. He knew they were about to inspect his home and collect his wife. The driver entered the vehicle and the escort took the front passenger seat. Once he was in place, the vehicle left the residence. Beck watched and called his wife's name as their home disappeared into the distance. Defeated, Beck sat back in his seat. It wasn't the normal soft leather-covered kind either. It was a hard, durable, molded plastic seat.

"Where are you taking me?" he asked.

"You sit quiet," the soldier said.

"What's going to happen to my wife?"

"You no worry. We take care of her," he answered with a smug smirk stretched across his face.

Within minutes, the patrol car pulled up to a tall sally port covered in concertina wire. Bright security lights that were affixed to the gate posts and buildings made the compound look like daylight. Next to the gate was a brick building with a tiny metallic sliding window. The window slid open, then closed. The door opened, and a Russian soldier exited. He walked over to the driver, who showed the Russian his identification card. Once the sally port guard saw the card, he radioed the person in charge of the gate and it began to slide open. The car drove in and came to a stop as the gate behind them began to slide shut, enclosing them between two security gates.

Beck's heart was racing ninety miles an hour. He feared for both his and his wife's safety. He knew why he was here. He made a fatal decision to betray his brothers-in-arms when he saw that Operation A.R.C.H.I.E. was escalating and the mobile communications units began their broadcasts. Unable to fathom what would happen to his daughter, he told the Chinese about A.R.C.H.I.E., the group, and its location. They weren't happy knowing just that. They wanted the names and locations of every member of the group, starting with the commanders. He gave them what they wanted. Everything except the names and addresses of the members. He didn't know that. It was a security thing. Not knowing the addresses of the group members insured a lasting militia should the commanders be taken out of action.

When news of the explosion got back to Beck, he knew he had forgotten one very critical piece of information – the C4 that lined the walls of the sewer system they were using. It could only be assumed that the Chinese believed Beck double-crossed the CTS. Treason is a death sentence. But why were they bringing him here? The Americans grew accustomed to public executions. If he was to be put to death, why do it secretly? What would that benefit the invaders?

The soldier in the passenger seat got out and opened the door where Beck sat. He performed an aggressive body search on Beck as he looked at an orange-dressed labor force worker carrying a few items around for a Russian supervisor on the inside of the compound. Beck knew it was a Russian supervisor because Americans weren't allowed to supervise.

That was an esteemed position. Esteemed positions were reserved for Russian and Chinese leaders. Seeing the orange jumpsuit made Beck believe that maybe he was going to be imprisoned. Maybe he was going to be a lacky for the Russians or the Chinese. Beck's escort pushed him toward a gated doorway to the right of where they were standing. There was a second gate to the sally port, but they didn't use it. Perhaps because they had a single human delivery and opening the grounds for such a small delivery wasn't worth the risk. Security was tight.

Am I to be made a prisoner now? he thought.

The soldier and Beck were met by two more soldiers that grabbed Beck by the arms and escorted him into an administrative facility. The building was secure. It had multiple Chinese and Russian soldiers supervising both the building and the prisoners. After leading him down a couple of empty hallways, they arrived at an office door that was labeled, *"Dr. Fa Huang."*

The door opened. A nicely dressed Chinese man stood in the doorway. "Ah, come in Mr. Beck. I've been expecting you."

Kyle was alone in the darkness. He wasn't deaf, although he felt like he was. He could hear his own swallows, clicking sounds in his ears, and other little things going on near his eardrums, but every external sound was incredibly muffled.

He was able to keep hidden within the shadows of the houses, trees, and foliage as he made his way to the rendezvous point. It was way after curfew. He already had an impending death sentence but being seen running around after curfew meant being shot on sight. No questions asked.

A mile or two outside of town and down the back roads was an old rock quarry where most of the adults used to play as children. The place had been abandoned for years until recently, when they decided to use it as a rally point. Kyle was leery about making his approach, since their normal meeting location had been discovered, and they were ambushed. How was he to know if their rally point hadn't been compromised as well? He decided to take the long way around using the deep ditches that surrounded the quarry as cover.

Beneath the thick branches of the old trees that lined the ditch, the moon's light was scarce. Nevertheless, he crept along the length of the trenches, peeking his head up every so often to see if he could spot any members. Nothing. No one. The place was barren and void of people. Kyle's heart sank. He hoped that they hadn't been captured, or worse yet, killed in the explosion.

As he pondered his next move, he was startled by the touch of a man's hand on his shoulder. He turned around and pointed his rifle at the person. It was Roy Sterns, a militia member of the highest loyalty. Roy was a widower. His wife killed herself not long after the economic collapse.

The new socialist system meant a massive change in the distribution of healthcare. Since the government was in charge of authorizing coverage, his wife went to the back end of the waiting list. She suffered from clinical depression. The way the system worked, if you were elderly and unable to contribute to society, you wouldn't meet government standards for immediate treatment. This was also the case for middle-aged adults, like Roy's wife, Therese. Therese was physically healthy, but her illness didn't fit the standards test that would provide immediate healthcare services. Since her condition was not an emergency, or something that met the criteria for immediate treatment, the government placed her petitions for medications on a hold list, allowing others with more urgent needs to be attended to first.

After the suicide of his wife, Roy committed himself to

the resistance movement. He joined Trenton Beck's militia group, although he was to the right of Beck politically.

"I didn't mean to startle you," Roy whispered.

Kyle could barely hear his words, but recognized Roy's face.

"You scared the daylights out of me," Kyle said. He looked around briefly then back at Roy. "Where's everybody at?"

"Things aren't looking good, brother. Beck called a meeting right after the mobile communications units began making their rounds. He sent everybody home and told them to go be with their families. He gave a long-winded rah, rah, rah speech then said something insinuating that you, Lyautey, and Glaspy were risking too much and putting our lives in danger. The crux of his message was that we're no closer to independence – only death. He said he'd rather have life under tyranny than no life at all."

"Wow, he's got it backwards! What about the others?"

"I don't know, but they should've been here by now."

Kyle sighed and peeked his head up from the ditch. Still nothing. "Something's not right. At least Glaspy and Lyautey should have made it."

At that moment, the faint sound of a mobile comm unit could be heard in the distance. Both Kyle's and Roy's curiosity were captured.

"Sounds like they're at it again," Roy said.

"Let's head back to town."

Back in the city, mobile communications units were roaming the city streets. They were commissioned to carry the following message to every region of the area:

"This is a message from the Communist Totalitarian Society. The great President of Motherland China, the honorable Shi Tao, has worked tirelessly to bring civility and harmony to the American people. He has provided you with free healthcare, food, and jobs. He has blessed you with skilled leaders; made it possible for all Americans to be equal to one another and to exist in peace with the motherland. Now, due to domestic unrest and sustained attacks on the Chinese nobles overseeing this country, he has declared a state of martial law. Therefore, the people of America are being directed to stay in their homes, turn on their televisions, and await further instruction. Further insurrection against the CTS will result in swift and immediate judgment."

The message was a recording and looped back to the beginning. It was heard far and wide.

Roy and Kyle heard the message as the mobile comm unit drove away into the distance. Kyle's hearing had returned, but he had an earache. He looked at Roy. "I can't return to my home. It's lost," he told him.

Roy welcomed Kyle to come to his place. "I don't have much, but I do have a TV, if you want to see what's going on."

Kyle was more than happy to follow Roy home.

Beck was told very little about what was going on. He was securely restrained in handcuffs to the chair that he sat on. Dr. Huang was speaking with him about Chinese customs and culture. Everything Huang said to Beck was alien, except for the part where Huang told him about his daughter and wife back in Beijing. The bonds of love between a father and his children are fairly universal. Huang's wife seemed like a wonderful woman; beautiful, from the way he spoke of her. Huang's daughter was about the same age as Beck's daughter. The very daughter that was missing and undoubtedly in the hands of the Chinese authority. Huang's time with Beck seemed pointless. It was small talk, really. Beck had a sick feeling in his gut that he was being set up for something atrocious. He couldn't shake the feeling, but Huang's smile and charisma kept Beck engaged on a professional level. He was trying to find hope in that when Huang's phone suddenly rang.

"This is Dr. Huang," he answered, in a casual and professional manner. There was a moment of pause and silence before Huang said, "Thank you," hanging up the phone.

Huang sat behind an antique-looking desk, reminiscent of the Resolute Desk of the Oval Office. He leaned over it and took his sophisticated glasses off and pointed to the television screen behind Beck. Beck turned toward the dark screen. The man that was standing there reached up and turned on the television. It was preset to a closed-captioned station that was authorized for public viewing by the CTS.

"Mr. Beck," Huang sad, "I didn't bring you here for a chat, although I do enjoy your company. It seems the group you told us about does indeed exist but weren't where you said they'd be. It appears as if I sent twenty Chinese soldiers to their deaths. A catastrophe that I lay entirely upon you."

Beck watched the news channel. Mandarin words scrolled across the bottom of the screen. English was the primary language being used to relay the coverage. There was a Chinese man with a microphone at the scene of the explosion. He was followed closely by a news crew of sorts. They were unquestionably Chinese reporters, a branch of the Communist Totalitarian Society, not well known. Their official title was *The People's News.*

"*Good evening. My name is Lei Cheng, reporting to you from Twenty-second and Vine Street, here in Wood Pine, Virginia, where recent attacks against the Chinese authority have escalated. As you can see, the damage here is catastrophic, taking the lives of fifty Chinese soldiers. After a tip from a Chinese sympathizer regarding the whereabouts of American terrorists, the soldiers were sent into a complex labyrinth of tunnels to make peaceful arrests of the agitators. However, we later learned that there were in fact no agitators present in the tunnel systems where rigged explosives were ignited killing the soldiers. It was determined that the man involved in the setup was none other than a leader of the now diminishing American resistance, Trenton Beck."*

Beck's picture flashed up on the screen.

"Mr. Beck was later found at his home with his wife and daughter where a stand-off against the Chinese authority took place. We regret to inform the people of Wood Pine that after several attempts to negotiate with Trenton Beck, he eventually took the lives of his wife and daughter in an apparent murder-suicide. The People's Republic of China mourns the family's loss and sends their condolences. I'm Lei Cheng. Good night."

The man standing beneath the television turned it off and readjusted Beck so that he was facing Dr. Huang. Beck's face was red and puffy. His eyes were full of tears as snot rolled down his upper lip. He had nothing to say. He had said too much already.

"I'm sorry for your loss, Mr. Beck. As you can see, we do not tolerate traitors. You betrayed your own people and you betrayed your leaders."

Dr. Huang stood up and adjusted his dress shirt and tie. He looked at the soldier and nodded his head. Huang left the room and the soldiers aggressively grabbed Beck and uncuffed his hands from the chair, then re-cuffed them behind his back. They pushed him through the door. Once outside, he saw the bodies of his wife and daughter laying on the cold concrete. Each of them had a bullet hole in the backs of their head. The soldier that was standing behind Beck lifted his pistol and pointed it at the back of Beck's head. He pulled the trigger and Beck's body fell next to the bodies of his family.

Roy and Kyle watched the newscast from Roy's living room and immediately knew the story was Chinese propaganda and lies. Kyle knew for a fact that there weren't fifty soldiers in that tunnel when the C4 was detonated.

"All lies!" Kyle shouted.

"You would know," Roy said. "So, tell me, what's the real number?"

"I'm not sure. Fifteen. Twenty, maybe. Beck must've sold us out. He never showed up to the meeting. He was behaving funny at the last meeting he attended. Plus, if what you said is true, I believe he gave us up. The Chinese will never admit to losing a firefight to the American resistance. They fluffed the story to make it sound like they're the victims and we're the agitators."

"Sounds about right. We have to assume he told them everything then. The secret locations, leadership names..."

"If they got our leadership names, they'd have our addresses. If they have our addresses, then we're squashed."

"We can rebuild. That's why the membership doesn't give out their addresses – only commanders."

"Interested?"

"I'm all in. I have nothing left to fight for except my freedom. The good Lord gave me that and ain't no Chin gonna take it away."

"It's going to take time and a lot of work. If you're up to the task, here's what I need from you..."

15

By spring of the next year, the Texas resistance was regaining its foothold in key territories across the state. While the Chinese fought skirmishes for national landmarks (thinking they'd diminish American nationalism), the real fight was happening over strategic areas like farmland, water sources, oil refineries, and other valuable assets. The A.R.C.H.I.E. model traveled far and wide.

The ambushes on Chinese and Russian convoys proved effective. The resources that the American resistance collected over time added up to a greater picture. While the Americans would never be able to meet the Chinese boot for boot, they still had the advantage. The American military was stepping up and reorganizing across the country. Without a commander-in-chief, the Joint Chiefs of Staff consolidated their efforts and resources to work as a unified body to defeat the invaders. The most problematic part of the process was trying to anticipate the rogue militia groups actions. Sometimes they worked in concert and other times they were counterproductive. There didn't seem to be any real organization and communication between the various militia groups.

In a way, it benefited the US Military. In another way, it hampered organized attacks.

The global community backed China's efforts, although Russia was growing tired of suffering loss under Chinese leadership. Slowly, but surely, the Russians were beginning to back their assets out of the field. These actions only strengthened Chinese resolve. Back in Wood Pine, Virginia, Dr. Huang struggled to maintain control of his region. The Chinese government was growing tired of his inability to control the Americans. Huang's argument was that he wasn't the only regional director struggling to control the nationalists; others were, too. Under threat of death, Huang was ordered by President Shi Tao to secure the region immediately. Further delay would hamper progress and interfere with the timeline he had presented to the United Nations. An army of militiamen were staging an offensive against Huang's region of control and threatening the future of the CTS's hold on the territory.

In the previous weeks, the Americans had gained air dominance. The Chinese couldn't seem to achieve air superiority over the American Navy and Air Force. The US military was consolidating their efforts and focusing on the coastlines, keeping the Chinese from supplying their ground troops with much needed ammunition and food. The militias were working together to control food manufacturing plants and farmlands. In addition, they were slowly taking over the news station centers and broadcasting their own propaganda. The Chinese still had a grasp on certain territories, but they were quickly losing control.

Commander Kyle Vanhorn had already given the fire mission to his people. He looked at Sergeant Sterns.

"Ready to go, Commander!" Roy Sterns answered. Newly acquired mortars meant the resistance could reach out and touch the Chinese from a long, long ways off. The ground-based Chinese forces were helpless against them. Kyle knew that the fight that lay just ahead was going to be a tough one. It was one that he was all too willing to fight. He was a combat veteran and a proud American patriot. He was fully prepared to give his life for his country. Now that it was spring, he worried less about Faith and Kayla. They weren't too far from his position. This fight wasn't going to be just for Americanism; it was for the posterity of his wife and daughter. This was it. This was everything. This battle would determine his fate and the future of his family's freedom.

Commander Kyle Vanhorn took one last look around. He was in the rear with the field artillery. Not too far to his north, the Chinese military had a strong grip of the region. If the militia could release it by killing the regional director of the CTS, he could retire home and let the military take over.

"Fire for effect," he yelled.

The mortars came alive with each drop of an artillery round. The 120-millimeter mortars slid down the M120 cannon assembly and sent the projectile five thousand meters to their destination.

Dr. Huang was on the phone when several Chinese soldiers came running into his office. They were all shouting in Mandarin and it was hard to make out what they were trying to say, but the gist of it was that he needed to evacuate immediately. About that time, the sound of mortars could be heard as they cut the air toward the doctor's vicinity.

"Get down, get down!" one soldier yelled, as if ducking would save his life. A loud thunderous explosion was heard a few meters from his location. Dr. Huang stood from his crouching position and ran outside to see what was going on. A Chinese military truck caught the first mortar round. What remained of the truck was ablaze. Chinese men that were close to the truck died in the explosion and were lying on the ground.

"Zhing Wei, what's happening?" Dr. Huang asked the lieutenant.

"We're under attack, sir! The American resistance has artillery. We need to get you out of here!"

A second and a third round hit almost simultaneously in the compound, narrowly missing Dr. Huang's office. A fourth round hit the corner of the building. The percussion caused by the blast knocked Huang senseless. The lieutenant died in the explosion. Huang came to his senses and picked himself up off of the ground. He didn't even remember falling down. With a dizzying twist of his head, he surveyed the devastation. Somehow, he alone survived the fourth mortar. He looked around and saw soldiers who were leaving in their vehicles. With blood running down his face from a cut on his scalp, he began to yell at a captain that was leaving the compound in a troop carrier.

"Captain! Where do you think you're going?"

The captain's ears were deafened by the mortar explosions. After careful consideration, Dr. Huang reluctantly left his post. Doing so would be considered desertion by the Chinese government, but the way he saw it, he could hide in America as an American. His English-speaking skills were above average for a citizen of China and he was a studious man, adept to change.

"Where should I go?" he wondered. "No time to think about it now." Dr. Huang ran as the mortars continued to pound the compound.

The next day, Kyle and a large group of well-armed militiamen stormed what was left of the compound. They were met with light resistance. Nothing a few well-fired rounds from their rifles couldn't manage. When the smoke settled, they quietly walked around the compound and took note of the destruction. It was bitter-sweet. Their intelligence told of a military base. It was more like an internment camp with a military-occupied presence.

"No wonder we took it so easily," Kyle said.

Roy was still by his side. "So many dead civilians," Roy responded.

"We didn't know. They told us it was a military fort. There's nothing we can do now. Just look for survivors, I suppose."

"I agree."

"Call a formation together and get this place shook down. I'm going to go on in and have a look around," Kyle said.

Roy was happy to do whatever Kyle asked of him. He hadn't led him wrong yet. "Form up," Roy shouted out. The company of men and women came together in four columns of fifteen people each. "Listen up. What we have here is a solid-clad victory with a bitter-sweet ending," he said to them. "We won, and we lost. The enemy has been defeated, but the cost was great. What we didn't know was that civilians were being held here as prisoners. For what purpose, we don't know. We're going to break into teams of three and shake this place down. We're looking for survivors. American survivors. Keep your wits about you. Asian people can be Americans. Use your head. Think before you act. Do you have any questions?"

One man from the front squad raised his hand.

"Yes?" Sergeant Sterns asked.

"What do we do if we find a Chinese survivor?"

"All prisoners will be treated with decency and respect. Detain them and make sure you keep them secure. We'll work on identifying them and determining what manner of justice will be served." Sterns looked around. "Are there any more questions?"

The group was silent. "Then fall out and gather yourselves in teams of three."

Commander Vanhorn was already walking around the compound, perhaps out of a sense of duty. Perhaps out of a sense of pride. He wanted to take in the victory in his own way. He strolled into a room labeled, *Dr. Fa Huang,* and began going through the filing cabinets. He found a file tagged *Trenton Beck,* and opened it. It wasn't long before he discovered the truth of Beck's deceit.

He betrayed the fight against the reformed Communist Totalitarian Society in hopes of keeping his family safe. As if some sick twist of irony took over, his family died with him. Kyle didn't believe the story that there was a "stand-off" at his residence. He believed he was murdered by the invaders, but the truth may never be known. There were no records of Beck's death. Only a red stamp on the file that said, "Deceased."

"Help," Kyle heard a man say from behind him. The English word had a strong Asian dialect attached to it. "Please, I need your help."

Kyle pulled his pistol out and pointed it at the man. "Who are you?"

"My name's Chin Gibson. I'm an American like you. Please don't shoot."

The man was wearing an orange jumpsuit covered in blood. Kyle noticed it and asked, "Who's blood is that?"

"It belonged to another prisoner. He died in my arms after being mortally wounded by an artillery attack."

Kyle put his weapon away. "Come with me. We'll get you taken care of."

Kyle walked in front of the man, giving his back to him. The man quickly and quietly ran over to the antique-looking desk and pulled the middle drawer out. Kyle heard the drawer slide out and turned around. The orange-clad man had a pistol pointed at him. He pulled the trigger and shot Kyle twice in the chest. He then slipped away out the back door.

Roy Sterns heard the gun shots and ran with a team of men to the office where they found Kyle laying on the floor. He was bleeding from the chest.

"Get a medic in here, now!" Sterns yelled, with a fierce expression on his face. Two militia members hurried off in search of help. "Hang on, Commander. You're gonna be alright," Sterns said, trying to comfort his dying friend.

Kyle tried to talk, but he had a sucking chest wound and the bleeding was severe. His lungs were quickly filling with fluid. Even if the blood loss wasn't going to kill him, he would still drown.

Kyle looked up at his friend Roy and clumsily reached into his pocket, pulling out two items. One was a picture of his wife and daughter. The picture was from happier times; from back before the collapse and the invasion. They were on a beach and all three of them were smiling.

The other item was a Purple Heart.

PART III DITCH OF THE DEAD

Written by L.L. Akers

16

DAVID, the leader of a teenage Freedom Fighter team of six kids, sighed heavily. His new recruits were down in the dumps. Some were hungry. Some were tired. Some were terrified.

All were missing their families.

Some of their parents had been executed for one ridiculous crime or another, and some had been taken prisoner by their new Chinese overlords. Some were still at home, forging ahead in their new version of reality, one nightmarish day at a time, hoping one day that their family might be reunited.

The Chinese had come, in the dead of the night, beating on every door, kicking them in when they weren't answered quick enough, and dragging out all the children they could find—screaming for their mothers the whole way—carting them off to child labor camps beneath a tsunami of tears.

The children were also used as pawns to keep the Americans in line. Bars and chains weren't necessary when faced with threats, bribes, and promises of their children, running freely from the lying tongues of their enemies. Bribes promising visits with their kids in exchange for turning in their fellow man for hoarding so much as a biscuit or a slice of bread over their assigned rations, or for violation of any other crazy law, or even to squeal about a possible pregnancy, which would result in the 'Chinese OutReach Program' escorting the mother-to-be to an undisclosed location for 'special care,' where the baby would unfortunately not survive childbirth for some unexplained reason.

Veiled threats about their children worked to squash insurgency, too. One cross look toward a 'supervisor' as the Chinese were called, and a clipboard was quickly produced, checking the name of the American's child so they could be sure to use it for maximum shock and effect in their taunts. No one wanted to hear their own child's name upon the tongue of these devils.

When the Chinese had invaded the American homes, they'd split up the children. Any child under the age of thirteen went one way, and thirteen and over went the other way. Even solace betwixt siblings was banned by the heartless monsters—their enemy.

David looked out over his team.

The new recruit stood strong and ready with a look of determined, but contained rage on her face. She removed her dark sunglasses and met his eyes with a steely gaze.

Brooklyn.

She looked like she was a force to be reckoned with: her almost-white blonde hair, a ramrod stiff back, balled up fists, and the lightest blue eyes he'd ever seen, that were filled with fire. Her fury made her five-foot five frame look ten foot tall and bulletproof. At sixteen years old, Brooklyn had the determination of someone three times her age.

Her anger was for the loss of her parents. They'd refused to give her up, as she'd squatted—hidden—in the middle of a round-bale of hay, hastily thrown together around her, listening to their screams from the back yard.

Earlier, when they heard the Chinese making their way down their street, answered by screams and cries of her neighbors, her mother had begged, and received, Brooklyn's promise *not* to show herself, no matter what.

Brooklyn had told her story to David, sobbing on her knees, when she'd finally found her way to the Freedom Fighters, and asked to join their fight for her own revenge.

He'd swallowed down a knot in his throat as she told him she'd known exactly when the interrogation was over, and when the Chinese had given up on getting her whereabouts from her parents. She'd known at that moment that the camp would not be her parents new home, as was their hope when the Chinese had come a'knocking. The punishment for not producing a known child in a residence was swift and sure, so they knew in their hearts it would be carried out, even if they'd harbored hope for a reprieve to the concentration camp.

But she'd heard the finality in the Chinese supervisor's voice, when he offered *one last chance* to give her up.

Deadpan.

Angry.

Committed.

In that moment, she'd forgotten her promise, and jumped from the hay bale, running swift-footed toward the house, ready to give herself up at the last second to save her mother and father. How bad could it be, where they'd send her? At least there would still be *a chance* to be together if they were still alive, one day. Her friends would probably be there anyway. She wouldn't be totally alone.

But she'd been too late.

Before she could reach the stoop, she saw them through the glass door. On their knees, looking out at the yard, holding hands. Their faces wore identical countenances of peace. They'd made their decision.

Her eyes had met her mother's, as the supervisor held a gun to the back of her head, and Brooklyn had clearly seen the goodbye painted on her face and the reminder of her promise reflecting back at her through her mother's silent tears. It was what she'd truly wanted. She'd made Brooklyn swear it on a Bible, over and over.

She'd dropped to her own knees in the dewy grass, one hand over her aching heart and one over her mouth, smothering a scream ... and she'd silently nodded her goodbye, and then kissed her own hand, weakly throwing the kiss to her mother, hoping she could somehow feel the love it contained.

Her mother had given a slight nod back, not able to return the kiss for fear of giving Brooklyn away to the supervisor.

The gunshot had split the air, nearly stopping Brooklyn's heart, too. But she'd forced herself to repeat her goodbye to her father, watching one lone tear trail down his face as he'd given her his special wink, one last time, nearly choking on his own grief through his bravery.

His hand had still grasped the lifeless fingers of his dead wife, who lay face-down beside him on the floor, as he'd struggled to stay upright on his own knees. His eyes had said "Go," and she'd blown him a kiss, too, and then dragged herself up as quick as she could, running like the hounds of hell were after her, hoping to outrun the sound of his life being extinguished.

Now she stared back at David, her new Chief.

David almost cringed under her stare. He was only one year older than her at seventeen, but she gave him full respect as her superior and mentor, in her father's absence. It was a heady feeling, to hold her life—and those of the other four kids—in his hands. He hoped he was ready.

He could see in Brooklyn's eyes that *she* was ready for her first mission. She was ready for blood.

He hoped she wouldn't be disappointed to find out it didn't involve spying or killing, or setting traps for the Chinese demons.

Not this time.

This time, they were doing something dangerous and disgusting, but necessary.

They were returning honor to a man who'd served his country, but came home only to ultimately find himself wandering lost, and homeless.

A man who'd had *everything* stripped from him, even before the collapse and the invasion.

A man who'd lived on the streets like a pauper, but treated his fellow brothers and sisters like queens and kings, providing them food and shelter as well as he could, when the Chinese refused to do so.

A man who'd been shot down for it, like a dog in the dirt.

David squeezed his fist, feeling a sharp poke to his palm, needing to feel a small measure of the same pain that this special man had endured.

They were to brave the Ditch of the Dead—a place of their worst nightmares—where they would look upon their family, their friends, their neighbors. They would sort through the piles and stacks of empty shells of their people until they found him.

He opened his hand and gazed at the Purple Heart, flipping it over and memorizing the number, and then stepped over and pinned it to Brooklyn's shirt. She stared down at it, running a finger over its edges.

David cleared his throat. "This is our mission, and Brooklyn is the keeper of the heart."

All eyes turned to Brooklyn.

He nodded solemnly at her. "Wear it well, soldier, with as much bravery as its rightful owner did, until we can return it to him."

He looked around at his young, tired team. "Let's move out."

While America still had heart—so would this man they sought.

Their mission was to return Archie's honor to him: his Purple Heart.

17

Special Forces veteran, Sergeant First Class McMinn, grumpily brewed his chicory roots over the open fire, wishing once again, as he did every morning, for a cup of real joe.

His dog lay stretched out beside him, his nose on his paws, giving him a sad look, hoping for something more than the two deer jerky strips he'd already scarfed down. McMinn shook his head no, and held his hands up in the air, feeling like the world's worst blackjack dealer, and received an almost-human guilty look in return, followed by a long whine —and not from the dog's mouth.

The dog had broken wind.

McMinn chuckled and reprimanded him. "Dammit, Shithead, I know you did that on purpose. I can't give you food anytime you beg, boy. Just be happy I saved you from *becoming* food."

The Chinese had taken so much from America.

Life. Guns. Freedom. Food. Family. Pets.

And so much more.

Most of their reasons for living, actually. But to McMinn, a lone-wolf of a man who didn't need what most did, the loss of his coffee was what perturbed him to no end. It ranked up near the top of his list, and it pissed him off that the enemy kept him from it.

He didn't miss his car, or his house. Or his big-screen TV. He could live without his queen-sized bed and a fluffy blanket, and definitely that damn spying smartphone. He'd tossed that aside within minutes. No, it was the simple things that he missed the most.

His coffee.

Clean socks.

And good healthy dog food that didn't make his dog fart.

When the collapse came, McMinn had topped off his bug-out bag, adjusted his rig, grabbed his M14, and hauled off on foot without hesitation, his loyal dog alongside him. He'd already been in war-torn countries, he'd soldiered through economic collapses, too. He and his team had been right in the thick of it and dealt with the after-effects as well. They'd torn down cities and rebuilt cities. They'd mowed down humans and saved humans.

He'd seen bad things.

Lots of them.

He'd *done* bad things—but all under orders.

He had worn the uniform, followed their orders, broken down his body, and had served his country well with every fiber of his being, sacrificing almost everything, until it'd nearly broken him.

But he'd survived.

He wanted no part of it again.

McMinn had made his mind up long ago, if and when the balloon when up—any balloon—he'd live his life out in peace, alone. Well, almost alone. No more fighting for him.

Having been counting his days to retire from his *second* career, after first retiring from the armed services, he'd almost welcomed the shit hitting the fan.

Finally, a do-over.

The country had gone cuckoo-banana-pants, in his opinion, and so far over to crazy-town that only a reset of this magnitude would ever set it back to balance. He'd almost been waiting on it. Let the economic collapse come. He didn't need money to live. He'd be fine.

He'd relished the thought of stepping off into the woods, away from the rat-race, and living off the land awhile. It would be an extended vacation for him and his dog.

Or so he'd thought.

But what he hadn't counted on was the invasion that followed the collapse. Soon, hordes of the skinny little bastards were surrounding every American, with not enough warning to fight them off, due to the first crippling blow that had been dealt.

The old quote of *behind every blade of grass* had been turned on its head ... because behind every blade of grass *now* was a damn Chinese.

He'd watched in horror from his sniper rifle scope as one small town after another was taken. Families divided, men beaten, women treated as slaves—and worse. There was no way he'd wear their ridiculous jumpsuits, their prison-style-shoes, or do their menial jobs for a slice of bread, topped with green cheese and paper-thin meat, and a freaking rotten apple, if he was lucky.

And he was only one man. He couldn't fight them alone.
No.
Their home was here.
It was there.
It was everywhere, now.

They stayed in one place until the hunting was no good, or the danger was too close, and then they moved on; and they usually ate like kings while they did it, foraging off the land and killing small game. McMinn enjoyed the nomadic life, the solitude, the open spaces. Especially after hearing the tinny screams traveling on the wind most every night; screams of victimized Americans.

Sometimes he wondered if they were even real ... or just stuck on repeat in his head, echoing through his ears—a phantom call for help.

He shook his head hard.

Nope.

Not his circus.

Not his monkeys.

He was *not* getting involved.

His hero days were over.

McMinn shook off his thoughts and got back to his own breakfast. Liquid only for him today, and then he'd gather and hunt more food for later. Using a bandana, he strained the dark brew and took his first sip of the day, cringing at the bitterness, and mumbling another string of curse words under his breath.

A branch snapped faintly and he and his dog both froze, listening.

"Shithead, hide," he commanded. The dog immediately rose up and crept silently into the woods, behind the first big tree he found and lay down with all four paws tucked beneath him, his ears pricked and his eyes watchful, waiting for his master to follow.

Quietly, McMinn dumped his brew over the small fire, gathered his backpack and gun, and melted back into the woods behind him, silent as a ghost.

Within a moment, a small party of teenagers came into his field of vision. They were stealthy—for kids. Other than the one tell of the twig that gave him the warning, a sound so faint, most would never have heard it, they were a sneaky bunch.

He watched in admiration as their young leader used

hand signals to move his troops, because that was what they surely were: a band of soldiers, albeit a *young* band of soldiers. Six of them in all. Four boys and two girls, ranging in age from probably fifteen to eighteen, at his guess.

The kids had weapons even. He smiled at that.

To hell with the enemy. Go ahead, take our guns ... you'll still see the American spirit fight back in the young and the old. *Take that, assholes.*

The young women — the younger one surprisingly wearing a Black Hawk tactical vest with a morale patch reading DD12 — were downright pretty and were also armed. In all, they had a ball-bat with nails protruding, wrapped in barbed wire; a few spears; a homemade bow and arrow; a slingshot; and a tomahawk.

Each one of them had a nice sized fixed-blade knife strapped to their side, too.

McMinn relaxed and slid down from his squat into a sitting position, leaning against the tree. He'd let them pass and go on their way. They'd survived this long, so they didn't need him. They seemed to be focused on something and doing fine. He wouldn't spook them.

As they moved, one by one, into the stand of trees, he lost sight of them. They blended in and disappeared easily.

"At ease, Shithead," he mumbled low.

He sent a prayer up for the kids and stretched, considering a nap, when Shithead let out a low growl. McMinn turned to look at the dog.

Shithead wasn't at ease.

McMinn hopped back up to his haunches and gripped his gun. Something caught his eye coming from the same direction the kids had come.

Chinese.

Two of them, even stealthier than the teenagers had been. The damn kids were leaving a trail somewhere, and the

Chinese had sniffed them out, like dogs on rabbits. It would only be moments before they were caught.

McMinn violently shook his head, sucking in his lips.

Dammit.

He knew *exactly* what would happen, as if it'd already played out.

He'd seen it before.

The Chinese wouldn't drag all these kids into camp. The had plenty of men and boys to order around now. It would just be four more hungry mouths to feed.

Maybe he was wrong—maybe they *would* attempt to take them all. But he'd seen the determined look on these kid's faces. They wouldn't go easily. There would be a fight. Americans that were brave enough to stand up, even if they had to hide to do it, were Americans that followed the old ways of protecting their women. These sorts of traditional Americans would respect their women, and give them equal treatment, but when the rubber hit the road, they wouldn't stand for what those girls were about to endure. They'd fight to the death and sacrifice themselves first.

Real men would.

And these boys looked as though they were well on their way to being real men.

But they couldn't win against speeding bullets.

Someone was going to die today.

18

David stopped, holding his fist in the air.

His team stopped behind him.

Was that a noise?

Sounded like a dog ...

He signaled his team down and they all knelt in the brush a moment, listening. He didn't hear anything else now; must've been a trick of the wind.

He put eyeballs on each of his five men—and women—noting they already looked tired. They'd need to take a break soon, but he had a bad feeling about this spot. Giving one more look around, he stood and signaled them forward again, when suddenly, shots rang out.

The team scattered, taking cover.

All except Jackie, who had been bringing up the rear.

Jackie screamed and crashed to the ground.

David's heart jumped into high gear as he watched his friend try to get up and run, then fall again, grab his leg, and drag himself to concealment, his leg blooming a bright cherry red.

"Jackie!" David yelled. "You hit?"

That was a stupid question, David thought. Of course, Jackie was hit. He'd seen the blood with his own eyes, hadn't he? He silently cursed his stupidity. They would all think he was an idiot. *No one will follow an idiot.*

His confidence was crumbling.

One man down and he didn't even know which way the shooting was coming from. How could he lead a team? Maybe he wasn't ready for this after all. Panic crept in.

Before David could make a decision on what to do, he heard two more pops, and then silence.

Again, he couldn't make sense of where the shooter was.

His head swiveled, and he turned completely around, eyes peeled. He saw nothing. When he turned back to where he'd started, one lone man and a dog stood twenty feet in front of him, holding a long gun.

David gasped.

An American?

Jackie got shot by an American?

He gripped his tomahawk tightly, ready to fight, but scared to death at the stern-faced man in front of him, and the dog that growled at his movements. *But ... an American?* He still couldn't believe one of their own people had just shot Jackie.

Crime between Americans had dropped to negative zero since the invasion. Especially with guns. If someone was lucky enough to have a gun and ammo, they hoarded it to turn on the enemy, not each other.

David gripped his tomahawk tightly and took a stance. "Everybody stay where you are!" he yelled to his team.

McMinn scoffed. "At ease, soldier. I didn't shoot your buddy. I just saved his ass. Yours, too." He ignored David's threatening stance and commanded Shithead at ease as well, then hurried over to Jackie. "Let me see it," he ordered.

"Then who shot him?" David demanded, looking around, still unsure if McMinn was a friend or enemy.

McMinn spared him a few words. "Chinese on your tail. They're dead. But you nearly all got smoked."

Jackie gritted his teeth as McMinn squatted down and pulled his Ka-Bar knife out. He split the leg of the boy's pants open, getting a good look at the wound. He whistled through his teeth, and looked up at David. "You got any medical supplies?"

David shook off his fear and slid his backpack off. "I've got some alcohol swabs, and a bottle of water," he mumbled, digging through it. "I have a shirt we can rip up, but it's not clean. *Ummm...*"

McMinn shook his head and removed his own pack. "Don't bother. I've got this."

Quickly, he ripped out his own first aid kit, and waved David in closer. "The rest of y'all get in here, too. If you already know how to do this, it won't hurt you to watch it again," he instructed. "No use wasting a GSW lesson on just two kids, especially since your buddy here probably won't remember a damn thing I'm about to show him, if he even sees it." He motioned at Jackie, who by now didn't care who was in front of him, or what they were saying. His eyes were squeezed tightly together in agony.

One by one, the other kids showed themselves, moving in to watch McMinn closely. The girls each took one of Jackie's hands, squeezing tightly, as he did his best to suck it up and put on a brave face for them.

McMinn's eyes slid right past the girls. He was sure they'd both caught their share of looks and leers, and he had no intention of making them feel uncomfortable in his presence. Besides, his focus was on Jackie, and what was going on around them.

"You," he pointed at David. "Watch our six while I take care of this."

David hurried away, leaving the other two boys with McMinn.

McMinn hurriedly cleaned the wound and then asked the kids who had the cleanest knife. One was handed to him and he sterilized it, then finished the job, causing Jackie to lose his fight with bravery and let out a girlish scream.

"Man up, soldier," McMinn barked at him. "You ain't even close to dying yet. It barely grazed you. You're lucky your shooter was a bad shot," he said as he wrapped the wound in his only clean T-shirt.

He stood up and called David back. "Y'all kids find me a long, sturdy stick. We need to make him a crutch."

While he instructed Jackie on how to clean his wound and re-dress it, and lectured him on what would happen if he didn't, the other five kids stepped away and hunted for a stick, finding the two dead Chinese.

They stood over the bodies with big eyes and open mouths.

"Holy shit. He killed them with one center shot to the back of the head," Egghead mumbled. The rest of the group hurried over with big eyes and open mouths.

"Who do you think that man is?" Hailey wondered aloud, a grimace on her face as she stared at the corpse. Hailey was a tough cookie, for a thirteen-year-old, but a hole in the head made her queasy.

Egghead poked his sliding glasses back up his nose. "I think he's a *real* soldier," he answered. "We need this dude, David. Ask him to go with us. He's got a gun."

"Yeah," Brooklyn whispered. "And he's a helluva shot."

"Shut up," David whispered back. "Don't let him hear you. We don't know this guy. Let's just get the stick and get the hell outta here."

David looked around. Scoop had disappeared again. The kid had a knack for it and he had to keep his eyes on him all the time, or lose him. "Keep looking for a solid, long stick, and if you see Scoop, tell him to stop taking off alone," he told Egghead.

Egghead tried to hurry away from the dead bodies, dropping his too-big glasses twice as he looked on the ground for the perfect limb, and nearly ran straight into McMinn.

McMinn gave him the dirty eyeball. "Hey," he said. "What's your name?"

"Egghead, Sir."

McMinn stifled a chuckle. "What's wrong with your glasses?"

Self-conscious now, Egghead gave them another push, sliding them up his nose yet again. "They're too big, sir. They weren't mine. I lost my own."

"Lesson number two. Never waste anything. Scavenge everything." McMinn stomped over to one of the dead Chinese, ripped his glasses off his face and tossed them at Egghead. "Here. Rinse 'em off and give 'em a try. You got a small head, kid."

Egghead caught the glasses and held them out with two skinny fingers. He shrugged. He stole a glance at the girls, and then wandered off to rinse off the glasses with a bottle of water, his boyish face crimson.

McMinn stripped the Chinese supervisors of their sidearms, too, and handed them both to David, who in turn kept one and handed the other to Brooklyn.

"What are you kids doing out here?" McMinn finally asked.

David straightened up to his full height, his face serious. "We're not kids. I'm nearly a legal adult. We're Freedom Fighters," he announced proudly. "We're on our first mission."

McMinn scoffed. "Any of you ever had any training as soldiers?"

"No, sir. No time for that."

"Any of you ever killed anybody?"

"No, sir."

"Anyone ever been shot at before?"

"No, sir."

McMinn blew out a breath and looked at Shithead, who was comically tilting his head from first his master, then to David, and back again, as though he too were following the questioning and very interested in the answers. "Let's go, Shithead."

David let out a big breath of his own, and looked around at his troops. His face didn't show much confidence, as McMinn made his way back out of the woods.

"Y'all be careful out here," McMinn muttered as he walked away, his heart heavy. These kids weren't ready to be out here alone. The Chinese weren't some benevolent overlords. They were killers, and he doubted these kids stood a chance against them. *Must. Not. Get. Involved*, McMinn told himself, pushing other thoughts out of his mind.

The sixth kid had wandered off alone, but finally reemerged carrying a handful of mushrooms just as McMinn was leaving. He cringed as the kid made to pass him, and he saw the kid had written something on the left breast of his shirt with a black sharpie: "Scoop."

He hoped that wasn't his name; but it looked like it. *Never give up your name to the enemy,* he thought. He shook his head.

"Look at these," Scoop said, proudly showing off his mushrooms. "Anybody want one?"

McMinn slapped them out of his hand as he walked by. "Eat that shit and you'll wish you were dead," he grunted.

He walked away, guilt pinching his conscience. He wasn't sure what asshat had set these kids out on a mission, but they weren't ready. Nowhere *near* ready. They weren't even prepared with food. They probably wouldn't be making it home—whatever sort of home they had—alive. His eyes filled up. So many lives lost in this war, without even a chance to fight. These would probably be six more.

It was a damn shame.

But not my circus, not my monkeys, he reminded himself, walking faster.

Behind him, he heard David speak to his troops. "Look, we'll find something to eat after we get that Purple Heart pinned back on." There was a pause. "Let's move out," he ordered his team.

McMinn stopped in his tracks. "What did you say? What *is* this mission of yours?" he called out over his shoulder.

David hesitated in his answer.

McMinn held stock-still, still giving them his back. "Answer me now, soldier, or find your head up your ass in two point four seconds."

19

Reluctantly, McMinn turned around.

Hearing Archie's story was all that he'd needed. It was one thing to look away from the rest of the world ... but to walk away from a mission of returning a Purple Heart—returning honor—to a brave, fallen brother? A mission that was doomed to fail from the get-go without him or someone else leading these kids?

He couldn't do it. Not to his brother.

He stomped back into the clearing and ordered the kids to line up, making sure they were all facing the sun beating down on them.

Thankfully, they listened. They passed his first test.

"I'll ask for your name and age. Tell me, but know I can't remember names for shit. If I say, 'hey you,' then you better answer me quick. I'm not babysitting a bunch of snot-nosed kids out here, and I'm not wiping your asses. Sounds to me like you asked for this mission. If I stick around to help ya, then you need to give me your undivided attention all the time."

The six kids all straightened up to their full height—all

but one who, not surprisingly, struggled to remain standing after just getting grazed by a bullet.

McMinn walked back and forth, a scowl on his face in front of the kids, giving them each a long study. They wiggled uncomfortably under his inspection. Except for Shithead, who took a spot at the end of the line. When he stopped in front of Shithead, the dog stared straight through his legs, frozen like a statue, for a long moment, until he couldn't stand it anymore.

His big brown eyes began to slide up, looking his master in the face, hoping for approval.

"Good boy," McMinn said under his breath, trying not to crack a smile, and then started back toward the beginning of the line.

Shithead wagged his tail.

"Name and age," he snapped at the first kid in line.

"David. Seventeen."

McMinn didn't spend much time on David, a stout boy packed with muscle; it was clear he was the leader of the bunch and probably the one he'd worry least about. He moved to the next in line.

"Name and age," he asked.

Egghead pushed his newly acquired glasses up his nose. These were too big, too. The kid really did have a small head. Small everything, actually. At probably six foot tall, he couldn't have weighed more than one-forty. He needed some meat on his bones worse than any of them. "I told you, sir. It's Egghead. I'm seventeen, too."

"*Real* name, soldier. I know your mama didn't name you after a damn egg!" he barked at the gangly kid, who visibly cringed in response.

"Egbert," he answered quickly, and kept going in a nervous explosion of words, "I'm named after King Egbert. A long time ago he ruled the West Saxons and formed a powerful kingdom that eventually achieved political unification in England," he sucked in a huge breath and continued, "... and my dad nicknamed me Egghead cuz my head used to be huge. I grew into it—and I guess out of it. But the nickname stuck." His eyes went to the ground, and then back up again. "Sir," he finished.

McMinn nodded, fighting down the urge to scream *TMI* at the brainiac. But, he wanted to toughen them up, not scare them to death. He nodded and then took one step to the right, stopping in front of a tall, athletic-built African American kid. "Name and age?"

"Maximillian, sir. But I go by Scoop. I'm sixteen," he answered easily.

"Basketball player?" McMinn asked.

Scoop rolled his eyes. "No, dude. Just cuz I'm black and tall and named Scoop don't mean I'm a basketball player. Racist much?"

"I didn't know *basketball* was racist. Thought it was *American*," McMinn stressed the word American, leaning in to within an inch from Scoop's nose. "Now eat some *shut the hell up*, kid, because I don't give a shit if you're red, black, green or blue. When *I* fought for my country, we *all* bled the same color. I was asking because your name is *Scoop* and I can't see someone tagging you with a name like that cuz you like ice cream."

McMinn finished his tirade and took another step to the right, but Scoop tried to correct his mistake. "Sorry, sir, they call me Scoop because—"

"Save it," McMinn interrupted. "My give-a-shit don't give a shit anymore."

Next up was the kid on a make-shift crutch, and McMinn was impressed to see the boy standing beside his team, using the stick to lean on. He'd seen some men in battle not pull it together as quick as this kid had after being grazed by a bullet. While it wasn't life-threatening, usually, it did mess with your mind a bit.

He studied his face. Chinese eyes stared back at him, with no malice. Their Chinese invaders didn't discriminate against Americans. They hated them all. Even the ones who looked like they themselves did.

"Name and age?" McMinn asked, not as harsh as he'd been with the other boys.

"Jackie. Seventeen," he answered through gritted teeth, but still managed a half smile behind it. The boy had no accent at all. He was American through and through.

"Your parents born here?" McMinn asked, curious.

"No, sir. They're legal Americans though."

"What side are they on in this war?" McMinn had frequently exchanged tidbits of information with others like him, people passing through trying to hide from the Chinese and live their life alone, on the go. He'd heard of some Chinese Americans trying to play both sides of the field.

"They're on our side, sir," Jackie answered.

That was enough of an answer for McMinn. The boy clearly said, '*our* side.' He took another step to the right and came face to face with what had to be the youngest of the bunch. He raised his eyebrows at her. What the hell was this kid doing out here?

"Hailey. Age thirteen, sir!" she said enthusiastically, yet with a small voice. Torn up jeans were topped by an American Eagle T-shirt and a Black Hawk tactical vest. The black and white morale patch on the breast said *DD12*.

McMinn sucked in a deep breath, staring at Hailey, and then let it out with a sigh. He turned and walked back to the beginning of the line to stand in front of David.

"What the hell is that girl doing out here? She's thirteen. What're ya thinking, son?"

David ran his hands over his face. "Sir, she would've

followed us. She was adamant she wanted to be a Freedom Fighter and other than hog-tying her and devoting someone to watch her every minute, there was nothing we could do to make her stay. We tried. She's young, but she's scary-smart and feisty. She has a mission of her own and is waiting for someone to go with her. She wanted to prove she could do this ... to everyone ... to hopefully find a travelling partner."

McMinn nodded. He understood stubborn females. Understood that you could never understand them, that is. He'd tangled with his share and even a hardened soldier knew once a woman made her mind up about something, it was more trouble than it was worth to try to change it. He walked back to stand in front of Hailey.

"What's after this for you, Hailey? What is your *personal* mission?"

Hailey's eyes filled with tears, but she roughly swiped them away and swallowed hard. "I want to make it back to the Tennessee mountains, to my Pawpaw and Grandma's homestead. That's where my mom and dad are, too. I'm sure they need my help. I've got to get home."

"How'd you get stuck all the way out here?"

"Came with a friend and her parents to get a few books signed from one of the DD12 authors, sir." She tapped her morale patch on her vest.

"And that is ... *what*?"

"It was a Facebook group of twelve authors, the Dirty Dozen Post Apoc Army, but some were having an in-person meet-up when things went sideways."

"So, they have an army? For the apocalypse? If there was ever a *post* apocalypse, it'd be now. Shit has definitely hit the fan. Where is this *army*?"

"They're spread out everywhere. We all stayed connected online. It was a book group of readers who love post-apocalypse fiction; mostly preppers, homesteaders, LEO, and military. But with the internet and phones disabled, the only way to reach them now is by HAM radio," she answered, gloomily. "But my pawpaw is probably in touch with them through the DD12 CommsConnect, if the Chinese hasn't shut them down yet."

This girl's devotion to her family touched McMinn's heart. He hoped she'd find her family again. Maybe this would be his next mission, too. He'd always thought Tennessee was pretty country. He could always help her get there and then step off and live off the mountains for a while. Why not? It was as good a place to hide from everybody as any, maybe even better.

He moved on to the last kid in line.

Fast as a snake, the girl ripped her sunglasses off her face. Lucky for her, as McMinn was just about to pluck them off himself, and comment about the lack of respect. She pushed her white-blonde hair over her shoulder and stood at attention.

"Brooklyn. Age sixteen," she blurted out in perfect English, not waiting to be prompted. She squinted hard against the blinding sun.

This was the first time McMinn had been close to her. Through her squinted Chinese eyes, he saw they were very light blue. She was an albino, and from what he could tell, the sun was painful for her.

He stared at her for a moment, measuring her grit. The sun was shining right into her face, yet she tried her hardest not to blink, causing her eyes to water terribly. "Put your glasses back on," he gently told her, and moved to the last in line.

Shithead perked up and sat tall on his haunches.

McMinn almost laughed at the still serious look on his dog's face. "On your feet, soldier," he barked at the dog, who had been patiently sitting in line for more instruction, shouldered up to the last kid in line.

Shithead stood up on all fours and held his head high.

"Sit."

Shithead sat again.

"Play dead."

Shithead fell to the ground, his tongue hanging out the side of his mouth.

All the kids laughed, still standing at attention.

McMinn had only been trying to teach Shithead a funny trick when they'd practiced this before the invasion, but it'd already came in handy once. They'd been caught unawares and McMinn had to quickly shimmy up a tree with his backpack to avoid detection, leaving Shithead to fend for himself. He'd commanded Shithead to play dead and *stay* dead, which meant until he released him.

The Chinese had either been too full, or too lazy to bother with what they'd believed was a dead dog they'd walked past, and they'd both lived to see another day. Since then, McMinn practiced that trick, and many others, daily with Shithead.

McMinn jerked his head toward the shade. "At ease, soldiers. Let's get these Chinese into their birthday suits and then re-evaluate your plan for the Ditch of the Dead."

He walked away, with Shithead loping happily beside him.

20

McMinn spent the entire next three days training the kids and teaching them survival skills.

The first two days, he showed them how to feed and shelter themselves, and how to best use their weapons. They didn't waste any bullets, as they'd only found two full magazines on the dead Chinese men, plus the fully-loaded guns. McMinn trained them as well as he could without actually allowing them to fire.

There was food all around them, they just needed to know how to find it, and he kept them going from dawn 'til dusk teaching them one thing after another.

He taught them to harvest and cook chicory roots for coffee.

He showed them the best way to gather dandelions and dig dandelion roots, and several ways to cook them and eat them, including hot or cold. He pointed out the good mushrooms versus the bad mushrooms. He taught them how to pick and cook Prickly Pear Cactus pads and fruit, without ending up like porcupines themselves, and how to use them to stay hydrated. The kids were amazed when they discovered the cactus pads tasted like green beans when cooked, and the flowers had a refreshing fruity taste.

He showed them how to tap a tree for water when they ran out, and how to make sure they didn't leave the tree to die; and how to make a homemade filter to utilize the water from any creeks and streams they found. He showed them how to light a fire without a lighter, and how to build a one-log fire, even if your one log was wet.

He taught them to build an underground cook-fire, to avoid smoke detection as much as possible, and the kids were now proficient at building a small, natural shelter, too. They could break ground and have cover in thirty minutes flat, sometimes less, after careful study of McMinn's techniques.

By the time McMinn was through, not only had they broken through his tough exterior and took to calling him Uncle Mick—usually behind his back—but they all now knew how to set a simple snare, use the bow and arrow, in case one was injured and they had to pass the weapon, and how to spear a fish.

Scoop in particular aced the snares and traps, and he was a dead-on shot with the bow and arrow, as well as the slingshot. Soon, Shithead was retrieving the arrows that hit low enough, and bringing them back, again and again for the team, and bringing Scoop rock after rock to add to the leather pouch for ammunition, earning a pat on the head or a rub between the ears.

Everybody took a turn with every weapon, but they'd all found the jobs they were good at, too. Even Shithead.

As expected, Brooklyn was deadly with the ball bat. She was also very accurate with the slingshot, if only they could find heavy enough natural ammo to be of use.

Egghead was amazing with the spear, for fighting, throwing, and eating. He pulled out more than a dozen small fish from the creek. McMinn taught them how to make mushroom and fish soup, with a few onions and herbs they also foraged, and they ate well for dinner both nights. Egghead became the camp cook.

David was exceptionally good at almost everything, but McMinn was able to give him some pointers on tomahawk throwing, and he found Hailey also had a knack for that, as well as the slingshot. She was a smart kid who learned quickly.

He showed them all how to sharpen their knives on river rocks, and he made sure they kept them honed sharp.

Next, he taught them to fight.

He had to get the group to straighten up and get serious for a while as he and David danced around in a mock knife-fight. Hand-to-hand combat with a knife could end very quickly, and very badly. Not for the first time, he wished they had more than one gun. Knife-fighting was a skill not easily taught, especially in a few hours, but he did the best he could with the time he had, and he hoped they'd not have to test their shoddy training.

McMinn was a sniper, and planned to use his own skills in protecting these kids with his M14, if it was at all possible. The training on the weapons was hopefully for *after* they parted ways.

Following the knife lessons, it was time to learn to fight without their weapons.

He was more than a little surprised to find out Jackie was a black belt in several mixed martial arts. His parents had migrated from China, and his namesake, Jackie Chan, the movie star born in their country, was a hero to them. Their first-born was named for him and he'd eventually grown into the name, with a little push. He'd attended martial arts lessons since he'd learned to walk.

In spite of his leg wound, Jackie still managed to take McMinn down a few times, bringing the entire group to laughter; even McMinn, who'd lightened up, seeming to enjoy having something important to do once again, although he denied it and tried to grab back his gruff countenance as much as possible.

Shithead couldn't have been happier. He ran 'round and 'round, helping the young women when they were 'under attack,' by pulling at the pant legs of the boys and giving a ferocious playful growl.

When Jackie had taken McMinn down, Shithead landed with a thud on his chest, nearly knocking his breath out, and covered his face with slobber, as he had done each of the kids who hit the ground.

At night, Shithead cheated on him, snuggling up between the two girls in their shelter, until the wee hours of the morning, just before breakfast, when he'd crawl out and relocate to McMinn's side, knowing who the keeper of the jerky was.

Traitor.

He knew he and Shithead would be leaving these kids after this and going their own way. His only mission was watching that Purple Heart be pinned back onto a fallen hero, where it belonged.

These weren't his kids, and he and Shithead couldn't get attached to them.

Especially to Hailey and Brooklyn.

Against his will, all the kids had grown on him, but especially the girls. They'd already wiggled their way into that dark place that kept his heart sleepy and unawares, and shined unwanted light in there. They'd also cracked his smile back open—a smile that was hard to find since he'd left Special Forces and all that happened *over there* behind.

He'd chosen a solitary life for a reason. He'd decided to not marry or have children; to live his life mostly alone. He liked it that way ... didn't he?

But Hailey's own sweet smile looking up to him with the

twinkle in her eyes, and her unending optimism that she *would* get home to her family combined with Brooklyn's raw determination to fight like a man and bring vengeance upon the Chinese for her parents—which he found incredibly brave and admirable—he was having a tough fight with his need to keep everybody at arm's length.

But he had to admit, if only to himself, that these kids had taught *him* more than he could ever teach *them*. They'd taught him that just because he'd been there and done that, and wasn't *active* military anymore, a veteran was still an asset to this country. He could pass on what he'd learned to the younger generation. He could teach them to survive, and to fight. And he'd barely touched the tip of the iceberg with them on what all he knew. The longer he stayed with them, the better trained they'd be.

If only he could round up more veterans. They could train these youngsters, and even their parents; teach them everything they knew and then ... they could take their country back.

If only ...

McMinn took a break, leaning against a tree to catch his breath, deep in thought. If he *had* a daughter, he'd be hard pressed to choose which she would be like: Brooklyn or Hailey.

"Hey, Uncle Mick," Jackie dared to call him. "Want to wake up from your nap, old-timer? See what Hailey can do now?"

McMinn wasn't an old timer ... not by a stretch, but he was feeling quite ancient watching these kids with their never-ending energy. His head popped up, to see Jackie on the ground, with Hailey's foot atop his chest. With her hands on her hips, the thirteen-year-old beamed with pride at having put the much larger boy on his back.

Jackie stuck his tongue out and played dead, imitating

Shithead's trick. The boy was a ham, always being silly or making a joke, but he was also the most dangerous out of the bunch. Between the two of them, he and McMinn taught the other five kids as much as they could in one day about self-defense, evasion, and even how to incapacitate or kill their opponent.

By the third day, McMinn was ready to move on their mission.

21

McMinn raised his fist, and the kids all stopped as one, squatting down low. He dropped to the ground and crawled up the hill, looking down into a valley.

He took a long look and then unfolded the map.

This appeared to be the right road. The crude hand-drawn map only showed the barn that Archie was last believed to live in, which was ten miles past this spot, and an "X" with *Ditch of Dead* scribbled beside it. This place must've just been on the way; some sort of camp or outpost—but this was not the Ditch of the Dead.

They probably either just assumed that it was, or didn't know about this place on the way to Ditch of the Dead. It certainly wasn't on purpose, McMinn thought. The adults were probably given wrong information, or not enough. The fact was, no Americans returned from the Ditch of the Dead to talk about it. It was a one-way ticket; the eternal dirt-nap.

So, it was only a guess that it was out here, based on seeing the Chinese heading this way with prisoners; some dead, and some alive, but never *returning* with them.

But no dead bodies could be seen—or smelled—as far as he could tell.

McMinn waved the kids up, and they all shimmied the hill on their bellies, lining up beside him to peek over as well.

For the next four hours, McMinn and the kids rotated two teams. One team watching behind them, and the other team watching two small, squatty rectangular buildings at the bottom of the hill, seeing nothing but two plump, old Chinese women going in and out.

There were no bars on the windows, so it was doubtful it was a prison, but to further confuse them, four guards were posted at different corners of the buildings. At the top of the hour, the guards changed, and the previous guards would hit the latrine, and then step into a round, canopied hut, where they'd hear dishware clattering.

After the third guard change, McMinn waved the team down off the hill to formulate their plan.

"You sure you can do this?" McMinn asked Brooklyn, for the third time.

"*Yes, Uncle Mick,*" she answered sarcastically, while tucking her hair up into a hat. "Why aren't you asking Jackie the same question? Is it because he's a guy?"

She checked her weapon once more, like McMinn had taught her, and slid it into the holster she'd stolen from the dead owner of the gun.

McMinn's original plan was for them all to keep on walking. It was his belief the Ditch of the Dead was still this way, just further down the road.

But the kids didn't agree with him. They wanted to take a look-see.

It scalded his ass that they were ready to break off from

him, even under threat of him abandoning their mission altogether, because they believed the younger children *might* be in one of those buildings.

He'd even promised the kids that once they secured Archie's Purple Heart back to him, he'd return alone and find out. And he meant it. He didn't want these kids taking any more risk than they had to, and he also didn't want to risk that medal not being returned to its rightful owner either.

But, all but Brooklyn and Hailey might have sisters or brothers that they'd been separated from in there and, if there was a chance, they wanted to free them.

Or at least *see* them.

So, it was on to Plan B.

Jackie and Brooklyn, the two Chinese Americans, donned the uniforms and the guns of the dead Chinese supervisors that McMinn had killed three days earlier.

They were to sneak up behind the squat building, incapacitate the guards, and peek into the windows.

Whatever they saw, they were to return to the bluff and report to McMinn for further instructions. They were *not* to enter the building, and were not to use their firearms unless their lives were in danger.

If they *were* seen, it was McMinn's hopes that with their ethnicity and the uniforms of the enemy, they might just walk on by without being questioned.

Meanwhile, McMinn would be on the top of the hill, laying prone with his M14.

It was a fat chance.

But it was a chance.

Brooklyn's heart raced.

They'd scoped out the camp from every direction and so

far, they'd only seen four armed guards, three old Chinese women, and a goat that was tied up in a shed, laying on a pile of hay, with a stack of metal buckets beside it.

Sneaking like bandits, and then running like their tails were on fire, they snuck between the two buildings into a small alley and waited for the guards to walk around as they'd seen them do earlier.

The uniforms the kids wore caught the guards by surprise, up close and personal, leading them to unanswered questions, but lending them a small window of opportunity to dispatch the two men before they were fired upon.

The first building they'd peeked into was a medical facility of some sort. A metal rolling tray had an assortment of surgery tools next to a dirty gurney, covered in a blood-stained white cloth. It had an adjustable spotlight hanging over it that swung spookily in the empty building, casting a bouncing light on the inside wall that was lined with blood-splattered ice coolers ... ironically, it was the best American coolers on the market: Yeti and other top brands.

Each cooler was marked with a red marker in Chinese letters; thus, they couldn't read it.

On the other wall an ice machine stood alone with a metal scoop hanging from a nail on the wall beside it.

An apothecary cabinet was the only other thing in the room. Behind two glass doors, it was filled to the brim with bottles and jars of what appeared to be medicine, as well as stacks of gauze, tape, and white cloth.

There was one door with a padlock hanging from it. From the position of where that room should be, and where they were outside, they could see there was no window. The padlock had the key in it and was hanging loose and open.

She jumped down from Jackie's back, who had knelt on the ground to give her a lift up, and stared at the two Chinese guards, leaned up against the wall of the other building, checking to be sure they were still out cold. She wondered how long they'd be out. One was directly under the window of the other building she needed to look in.

"Can you move him without waking him up?"

Jackie easily dragged the man away from the window.

Brooklyn still couldn't believe she'd managed to knock out a full-grown man with only one day of training. Jackie had handled his much faster, but they'd both gone down, and Jackie had easily dragged his man over to Brooklyn's.

Jackie leaned them up together against the wall, side by side and then reached down and clasped one's right hand with the other's left hand, and pushed their heads together, turning them to face one another just a breath away. He stepped back and pointed at them, mimicking a Chinese woman's voice and saying, "Me love you long time, yes?"

He smothered a laugh.

"Stop it," Brooklyn whispered loudly at him. "Do you want to get dead?"

Jackie took in a deep breath and let it out. "Sorry. I goof around when I'm under stress. Come on," he said, and motioned her to the window.

He got on all fours and waited.

Brooklyn climbed up, using him as a step, and grabbed the sill of the window to balance herself.

She peeked in for a long moment and gasped. "Holy crap."

"What's in that one?" Jackie whispered.

"Babies!" Brooklyn whispered back. "The sign in there says, 'Chinese OutReach Program.' Those lying pigs ..."

The Chinese OutReach Program was supposedly a program for Americans, provided by their generous overlords, that helped pregnant women. The Americans didn't want it, but they got it anyway.

The Chinese said it was years and years of poor nutrition

that caused the American's to now lose nearly every child born. They blamed fast-food habits, junk food, loose women, and the use of dangerous pharmaceutical medicines. If they even heard a whisper of a pregnancy, the Chinese OutReach team immediately arrived to extract them from their husbands and homes to take them somewhere where they'd supposedly get fed better and taken care of with little to no hard work until time for them to give birth.

The only problem was each time the mothers returned *without* their babies, if they returned at all. They were not conscious for the births and, when they awoke, they were told their babies did not survive.

They were told their babies were *dead*.

No one believed this.

Brooklyn was now looking their lie in the face.

In *four* faces.

While the babies' eyes were covered with bandages for some reason, Brooklyn could clearly see the babies were *not* Chinese. These were American babies; two were African American with darker skin and thick, tight black curls atop their heads, and two were Caucasian—milky white skin tone, one with curly blond hair and one with bright red hair.

The babies were laying in crude excuses for cribs on bare, dirty mats. Their hands were covered with layers of socks, and she imagined that was to keep their fingers out of their eyes. She wondered what had happened to them.

There were no toys, no fuzzy blankets, no musical aquariums.

Clothed only in small, short-sleeve T-shirts, and what appeared to be a ripped-up piece of sheet pinned with a cold, sharp safety pin, their bottoms were wet, and worse. She could see the children desperately needed fresh diapers.

The babies were laying in their own filth, and shivering without even a blanket to keep them warm.

She couldn't hear their cries through the concrete walls and thick glass, but she could see their mouths open wide, each making a dark little anguished 'O.' They were all either terribly hungry, uncomfortable and scared, or missing their mothers.

Probably all of the above.

A tear ran down Brooklyn's face.

She missed her own mother.

"Hurry up," Jackie whispered loudly, struggling to hold Brooklyn up so long.

Brooklyn quietly hopped off. "*Shhh ...*" she said. "Here comes someone."

They both squatted down, staying quiet.

After a moment, they heard the door click shut. Brooklyn motioned Jackie to help her up again, and he moved to get on his knees, on all fours. She climbed up.

She slowly raised her head to look in the window. A chubby old Chinese woman came in with four bottles filled with milk.

Brooklyn watched as she stuck the first bottle into the red-headed baby's mouth, while the baby waved its arms around, frantically trying to grab at the food—or for human interaction—while she meanly swatted its tiny hands away. The baby sucked long and hard for only a moment before the woman snatched it out of its mouth and moved to the next crib, repeating the process.

"Omigod," Brooklyn muttered. Her heart clinched. These innocent babies were clearly starving and the brusque old woman wasn't giving them a chance to drink much.

She finished the two bottles between four babies, left them all red-faced and screaming for more, and then ignoring their needs to burp or be changed, she took the other two bottles to a rocking chair in the corner.

She fluffed up the pillow, sat down and removed the nipples, and drank them herself.

Brooklyn was livid.

She hopped down, noticing the guards were starting to stir.

"Hurry," she said, running for the woods that led them to the hill where McMinn lay on watch.

Jackie ran behind her only showing a slight limp from his injured leg.

22

McMinn listened to their report and then quickly led the team back down the hill, approaching the two downed guards just as they were coming to. He knocked them out again with one strong tap against their temple with the butt of his rifle.

David and Scoop each grabbed one man under the arms, dragging them into the empty building behind McMinn, who cleared the rooms first, and then ordered the kids to put the Chinese behind the door with the padlock.

Brooklyn passed her gun to Egghead, who stayed outside watching their six, and followed David and Scoop.

The door with the padlock was a storage room filled with rice, blankets, baby clothes, and ammo, and to the kid's sheer bliss: Pop Tarts.

Seems the Chinese weren't immune to the pull of *all* American junk food after all. *Someone* had a hankering for these flat American delights, filled with artificial flavors and sugar.

Shoving them into their pockets, while McMinn bit his tongue and watched the door, listening for any warning from

Egghead, the other kids quietly fussed and argued over the flavors: blueberry, s'mores, and strawberry, until McMinn hissed at them to *come on*, locking the padlock behind them, and leaving the guards behind and secure.

Before moving to the next building, he examined the blood-spattered coolers and the ice machine, and then looked at the metal cart with the surgical tools, and the bloody gurney under the light.

He had a suspicion he knew what was going on.

Careful to avoid the other two guards, he peeked out the door, and waved the kids behind him.

He tossed Egghead several packs of the Pop Tarts, receiving huge eyes and a smile in return, and then they moved on to the next building.

The door creaked open and he quickly cleared the one-room building, finding it empty, other than the babies.

He hurried over to the first child and lifted its shirt.

The child flinched at his touch.

Rage filled his head, and he moved to the next, and the next and the next, his body vibrating with anger.

His suspicions were correct.

These children's body parts were being harvested. A bandage covered a spot on each of them where a kidney had been removed, then probably put on ice, and auctioned off for a million bucks and flown to some rich asshole with more money than ethics for his own loved one or himself.

He was afraid to look under the bandages across where their eyes should be. He didn't know that he could keep it together if he found two black empty holes staring back at him from these infants. He ignored those for now.

McMinn pushed his rifle to hang behind him, and spoke to David. "Keep your eyes open," he said gruffly, and picked up the last baby in line, holding it close. His nose wrinkled in disgust, but the disgust wasn't for the baby or the stench, it was for the people who weren't taking care of it. Or not, as was the case.

Sadness stabbed him like a knife for the mothers and fathers caught up in this unfought war, who hadn't been able to hold their own children, but especially for the children who were missing the warm, loving feeling of being held and cherished by their parents; who missed the skin to skin contact, and all the spoiling and love a newborn child—any child—should have.

Squeezing his eyes together against the smell, he checked its nappy; it was full. And it was a boy ... McMinn's heart clinched as he brought the baby close to him again, ignoring the stench of unwashed skin, feces and urine. He softly cooed to the baby boy, and rubbed his soft, dark curls, kissing the top of his head.

Animals.

That's what these Chinese were.

Heartless animals.

McMinn looked up to see Jackie watching him hold the baby, tears filling his own eyes. Jackie swallowed hard and cleared his throat. "How can they do this?" he said, knowing exactly what McMinn knew. "I mean, my family is Chinese. We come from China originally. How can people be of the same origin, with possibly the same blood somewhere down the line, but be so different? So inhumane? I'm *ashamed* to be Chinese."

McMinn shook his head. "Don't be. You're not like them, and they're not like us. Blood doesn't make you family. *Heart* does. Look around you. Here's your family now, boy. Suck it up. Gather some things, we're not leaving them here."

Jackie hung his head low. "I would never do this, McMinn, not to *any* human, even if they were our enemy."

"No shit, man. We know you're not one of them. You've got nothing to prove. Brooklyn's Chinese, too; being like them in DNA doesn't make y'all *like* them. You're both one of us: *Americans*. Now get your head straight and your shit together."

A flurry of activity ensued. Brooklyn grabbed a rolling cart from the corner and she and Hailey filled it with blankets, clothes, bottles and whatever they could find. While they did that, the boys watched the windows and the door.

McMinn turned and looked at the cart. There was a wire shelf with a lip on it directly underneath. Room for more stuff. It would make it heavy, but hell, David was built like an ox anyway. "Hey, Scoop. Run to the other building and grab as much rice as you can carry. Stack the bags under the cart on that shelf. Find a carry-bag or something in there and grab as much of the medical stuff in that cabinet as you can, too. Diaper cream, antibiotics, whatever they have. But don't get seen," McMinn ordered. "Hurry! I've got one more thing to do before we go."

He turned to his task and very quickly changed four tiny diapers, not able to fathom leaving the children in soiled cloths one moment longer; he was careful to fold the top of the diaper over the cold, sharp safety pin so that it didn't touch their skin.

He looked over his shoulder to make sure he wasn't being watched before kissing each tiny head, speaking quietly to them, and gently rubbed their too-skinny arms and legs before placing them in the cart, atop the bundle of blankets. The babies had quieted at his voice and now-dry bottoms, even blindly reaching out to him again for his touch, their tiny limbs waving frantically in the air.

They were starved for more than just milk.

Jackie stepped over to the cart with his arms crossed, staring at the malnourished, bandaged babies once again. His jaw was clenched. He was stuck in his own head, doing nothing to help.

McMinn gave him a light slap against the noggin. "Wake up. Let's go."

He took the lead after giving orders. "David, push the cart straight back up that hill to where we were. Egghead, you trail David. Shithead is waiting for us. We'll all rendezvous there and two of us will take the babies to the barn that was on the map, while the rest of us go find Archie to complete your mission."

The babies began to cry. His head swiveled left to right and back again. "Scoop, you get that goat and Jackie you're with him. Watch his six. We'll need the goat for milk. Hailey and Brooklyn, with me."

Brooklyn was fidgeting with the babies. "Omigod. *Look at this!*"

One of the baby's bandages had slipped off of its eyes to reveal it still *had* eyes, but they weren't typical American eyes. Tiny stitches revealed recent surgery, re-shaping the eyes to look like their captors.

The baby looked around in wide-eyed wonder and then screamed in fright at the shocked eyes staring back at it.

Egghead cringed. "Dude. That's messed up."

They gathered around the cart and removed the remaining bandages. All four babies had been altered.

McMinn looked around at the horrified faces. He'd seen worse done to prisoners of war but not to *babies*. Not live babies anyway. Before he completely lost his shit and went to hunt down every Chinese he could find, throwing lead at them and possibly risking the lives of all these children, he needed to refocus.

He waved the girls behind him and took off, assuming his orders were being followed as given, when suddenly Scoop yelled out for Jackie.

Before he could react, Jackie had taken off back toward the buildings.

"Dammit, Jackie!" he yelled. "Meet us at the barn then."

He had an idea he knew where Jackie was going.

McMinn let him go without a fight; Jackie had demons of his own to purge, and something to prove to himself. This was his choice, and he was choosing to become a man—a real Freedom Fighter—or fail trying.

23

McMinn mopped his sweaty brow with his forearm and then cringed at the smell. His head was pounding. His heart was thumping.

But it wasn't the sea of dead bodies around him that was bothering him. For the first time in many, many decades, he felt something unfamiliar to him.

Sheer panic.

And it wasn't the fear of being caught in this God forsaken place of death, surrounded by a sea of faces frozen in horror ... it wasn't fear at all.

He'd faced walking into villages as the point of first contact, shirt off and arms spread wide, unarmed, and possibly facing his own death. He'd jumped out of perfectly good birds. He'd ambushed parties that had him outnumbered ten to one and rarely blinked an eye.

He'd eventually slept like the dead in war-torn countries with blood and bullets flying all around him, not even fretting whether he would, or would not, wake upon the dawn. He'd learned to squash his feelings, burying them so deep he'd forgotten what they felt like.

So, this ... this *thing* he was feeling, it was unusual for him. Foreign.

Worry.

Was it possible that in less than four short days they'd unknowingly broken down the walls around his heart, and made him actually *feel* something again?

Something like ... *love*?

He looked over at David and Brooklyn, who were also knee deep in rotting flesh, pulling, lifting, sorting, as though they were at the Goodwill looking for a pair of cool worn-out jeans.

But this was no bargain basement.

The strength these kids were showing, possibly looking into faces they'd known; now-blank faces that may have been related to them in some way, or friends, or neighbors, was amazing.

He was *proud* of them; another new feeling to him.

Despite the ugliness, despite the smell, the two kids stoically pursued their prize.

Archie.

He watched them with pride as they dug in, not shying away from the dirty work, and probably the hardest thing they'd ever had to do, looking for a hero.

When all along, *they* were the heroes.

McMinn took in a deep breath and coughed it back out. He was glad Scoop had confiscated a jar of Vicks when he'd robbed the apothecary cabinet. They each had a generous smear of it under their noses and even so, the stench was stomach-curling. Without it, it may have been unbearable.

But yeah, watching those two kids right now, his heart swelled with all sorts of foreign feelings ... topped with worry.

His worry: the group had split.

He'd sent Hailey and Egghead, with the babies, on toward the barn that that was marked on the map. It was the group's understanding that Archie had once lived at that barn. Since he'd been captured and killed in town, it was possible the barn was still secure.

When the team arrived at the top of the hill, Shithead had met them, his happiness at being reunited with his master and the kids unbridled. He'd hopped around, barking and spinning in glee, and then curiously sniffed the cart that held the babies, jumping back when one let out a cry.

After that, Shithead promoted himself to *Protector of the Little Humans*. For a moment when McMinn, with Brooklyn and David, split paths from the babies, pushed by Egghead and Hailey, it was as though Shithead had to think hard about which way he wanted to go.

McMinn had breathed a sigh of relief when Shithead eventually fell in step beside him.

But Jackie hadn't returned to the hill. And Scoop didn't stay.

Within moments of their return, the team had heard a *pop, pop, pop*, and they'd all froze.

But whatever had happened, it was too late.

McMinn now had a mission of his own.

To get the majority of the kids, and the babies, to safety.

If he had to drag his feet through a swamp of blood and guts and empty stares to complete his mission, he'd do it. But he wouldn't sacrifice another one of them. He'd made a decision to go on without Jackie.

Scoop didn't like that decision—he'd turned tail and ran back down the hill after his buddy.

Very admirable, but it didn't change McMinn's mind. The numbers didn't lie. Six lives weighed heavier than two. They all took off, him hurrying both parties along, and hoped to see Scoop and Jackie again, one day, but praying for their souls in case he didn't.

Brooklyn gave a low whistle, rousing McMinn from his musings, and he and David turned in alarm.

The American worker that they'd bribed with a bag of rice to give them three orange jumpsuits and turn his head, was coming back.

And he wasn't alone.

Luckily it was just another American worker with him. The Chinese didn't get their hands dirty here. According to the first man, who more than happily traded the rice for allowing them to look through the dead, they rarely ever saw their Chinese bosses. There wasn't anything here to eat or steal, so they left them unattended to tend to the dead; to unload any new bodies that were brought in and throw them into the ditch each morning.

Funerals and burials were a thing of the past in the *new* America. The Chinese considered this a waste of time and money if it was just an American life that was lost. Once a month, the men in orange suits would burn the stacks of bodies and when that had burned down and the smoke cleared, they'd continue to pile them on, as they were told.

The two men approached them. The new man, elderly and frail, scratched his bald head, tufts of white hair blowing in the wind around his ears. "What in tarnation are y'all doing in there?" he asked, with an incredulous look.

McMinn's hand hovered over the sidearm he was hiding; one re-confiscated from the kids. David had the other one and McMinn gave him a slight nod to be on the ready, before he answered, "We're looking for someone."

"Why would you need to find them? We check those bodies before we dump 'em. There ain't no valuables on 'em."

"We aim to fix that," McMinn said. "Show him, Brooklyn."

Brooklyn turned to the men and unzipped her jumpsuit, showing them Archie's Purple Heart. "We came to pin this on

Archie, and if it's possible, we'd like to take him with us and give him a proper burial."

The old man spread his mouth, showing off no more than a handful of teeth, and laughed. "*Archie?* Archie the homeless veteran that helped feed so many of us? *That's* who you're looking for in the Ditch of the Dead?"

He slapped his hand on his legs, with a huge belly laugh. His friend laughed along with him.

McMinn didn't find it humorous.

He pulled the sidearm, and pointed it at the two. "Not sure what you find funny, mister, but I'll ask that you leave us to it. This is a serious mission for these kids. They aim to give that hero back an honor he earned."

The men held their hands up, palms out. "Wait a minute," Toothless said. "You should've mentioned his name when you showed up. You won't find Archie in that mess. You head out to the old barn where he used to live, and you'll be able to re-pin that medal."

The other man nodded his agreement. "Can we keep the rice anyway?"

24

"He's coming!" Brooklyn yelled to the others.

The kids all ran outside the barn, each holding a squirming baby, their hope and anticipation tingling through the air. The goat followed them out, adding its own loud racket to the excitement. They'd been waiting on McMinn—having full confidence that he'd return—for three days.

After the news from the men in orange, McMinn had sent Brooklyn and David to the barn to meet up with Hailey and Egghead and the babies while he headed back alone to the Chinese outpost to see what had happened to Jackie and Scoop.

He just couldn't leave those kids behind.

Dead or alive, he *needed* to see if there was anything he could do once he felt the rest were somewhat safe.

Shithead came rocketing down the dirt road first, which was what had given Brooklyn the head's up that McMinn would soon be following. She'd been sitting outside watching almost since their arrival, barely sleeping or eating.

The dog made his rounds, jumping up and greeting

everyone, and getting rubs and scratches and pats on the head in return.

His master's head then topped the hill, carrying something across his shoulders. He walked heavy and slow under his burden with Scoop trailing behind. He squinted his eyes as he approached the kids, his heart swelling to see all four of them, with all four of the babies, all in one piece.

Scoop ran ahead to his friends, hugging them in turn, and then ran back to meet McMinn again with David in tow.

David took McMinn's heavy burden, giving him a much-needed rest as he finished his journey, and after suffering through the rest of them wrapping their arms around him in a huge hug that watered his eyes, McMinn followed him inside the barn, with the whole crew behind them.

Gently, David laid Jackie on a blanket atop a pile of hay and then stood back, looking at his injured friend. He was alive, and that was all that mattered, but now in addition to a scar on one leg, he'd have another piercing his other leg.

"Did you get 'em?" David asked a weak Jackie.

Jackie nodded and smiled. "Every one of them, but not before they got me. Lucky for me though the Chinese are terrible shots."

He held up a weak fist and David fist-bumped him and turned to Scoop. "How 'bout you? Any injuries?"

Scoop shook his head. "Only my pride that this old man is stronger than me," he said loudly, hoping McMinn heard him. "Took me hours to drag Jackie's ass up that hill ... then y'all were gone. Uncle Mick carried him the whole way here and barely broke a sweat."

They both looked at McMinn, who was currently sitting on the hard-packed dirt floor, four babies squeezed onto his lap. They gathered around him.

Embarrassed to be caught in such a moment, McMinn swiped at his eyes and cleared his throat. "So, did you find him?" He looked around, wondering if the man had been buried under this very floor where he sat.

"Yup," Brooklyn answered with a smile. "Archie!" she yelled.

A grouchy, old voice answered. "What?" and then Archie came wobbling through the back door, wiping his hands on his dirty apron. He wore a clean bandage mostly covered with a bandana around his own head.

McMinn gently handed the babies to the kids, and then stood up to meet the man with a salute. "Well, shit. You're alive," he said in surprise. "The men at the Ditch of the Dead didn't say *that*. They just said we'd find you here."

Archie laughed. "Loyal bunch they are. They're the two that pulled me out of that ditch. Saw I wasn't quite dead yet and patched me up. I owe them my life; what's left of it, anyway."

He noticed Archie wasn't wearing his Purple Heart. "And your heart?"

Archie shrugged. "No worse for wear. It acts up every now and again. Flops around like a fish in there until I sit down and rest a spell."

"I meant your Purple Heart. That's what the mission was. To return your Purple Heart to you. It's really important to these kids to see that pinned to your chest," McMinn explained.

Archie reached into his pocket, took out the medal and stepped up to McMinn, pinning it to the shirt of the younger man. "Here's where I'm gonna have to pull rank on you, soldier. And the kids agree with me ... you're the hero here."

PART IV: MANDY'S REVENGE

Written by Boyd Craven III

25

"Who wants to do it?" McMinn asked.

"I will," Brooklyn said, pushing her way through.

"No way," Egghead told her. "You're not —"

"It can't be any of the younger kids. The only adults working there are sympathizers and nobody else is old enough or smart enough to get the distraction we need so we're not mowed down."

"Nobody's going to get mowed down," McMinn commented, lying on his stomach in the tall grass, looking at the work camp below them with a set of binoculars held to his eyes.

Their guerrilla war against the CTS had started picking up steam, and as the resistance grew, so did their numbers. There were just as many kids, as well as parents, hopeful of being reunited with their loved ones; some, they hoped, were inside.

Foster homes had been found for the few babies that had been liberated in the past, as the group moved on. Their advance wasn't nearly as well-known as A.R.C.H.I.E., and the stories surrounding it, but it moved with them and grew.

McMinn could feel it pressing against him as he lay prone watching.

"Trucks are coming up," Brooklyn said. "Time for me to go and —"

"I'll do it," Egghead interjected, a tremor in his voice. "I'm old enough, I'm big enough and I'm ... I'm smart and I can figure out how to get this diversion done. If you go in, Brooklyn, I'm worried that ..." His words fell off and both kids shuddered at the unspoken thoughts.

"It won't be safe in there," McMinn said rolling on his side before sitting up. "And you're not as good with your fists as she is," he added, nodding his head toward Brooklyn.

"If I do this right, no fighting will be needed," Egghead told him, his hands shaking.

Brooklyn looked at him, her head cocked.

"Why is it so important to you that I not go?" she asked him gently.

Egghead shrugged his shoulders and mumbled something unintelligible.

Brooklyn let out a dramatic sigh. McMinn looked between the two and saw both of them were scared. Hell, he was scared for whoever ended up going. He did think Egbert had the right idea though. He was smart and pretty clever, but he didn't have the same killer instincts that the girl had. Then he had a thought.

"Here," he said, pulling Archie's Purple Heart out of his inner breast pocket and pushing it into the boy's hand. "Hold onto this until we come get you tomorrow night."

Egghead gulped, then nodded, something in his gaze changing, hardening.

"I'll keep it safe," he said, his voice almost a whisper.

"You do that. Remember, the meetup spot is by those fuel tanks, but if you don't hurry, those trucks down there are going to pass you by."

Egghead got up and hugged Brooklyn quickly, blushing, then shook McMinn's hand and took off down the hill toward the main road. Brooklyn and McMinn sat down, neither of them feeling good about what they had just done.

"It should have been me going," Brooklyn said, breaking the silence as Egghead made it to the roadside, the convoy of trucks still half a mile out.

"This might be the place," McMinn said gruffly.

"Where they're experimenting on ...?" She didn't finish the thought.

"Yes," McMinn said softly. "We won't know until we get the files. I figure that's why Egbert didn't want you going. You being the way you are ..." His words trailed off as he took in her pale skin. "You might be put right into the breeding program."

"I carry the albino genes," she said quietly. "In their eyes, is that a good thing, or a bad thing?"

Both went silent as Egghead started waving his hands over his head in an X shape and then out wide in a Y, over and over until they could hear the brakes and air cylinders compressing as the column stopped. Several soldiers hopped off the back, guns out and ready. Egbert was roughly frisked, then led to the back of the transport truck at gunpoint and pushed in. The brakes were released, then the trucks drove to the gate of the facility and entered one by one.

"I hope we did the right thing," McMinn said softly, wishing his dog was with him, instead of back with the main group.

"I can always head to the gates and tell them I'm looking for a friend and they'll—"

"No, we're not going to let you get caught, too. If something happens to me, I'll need somebody I trust to carry on ... and keep Shithead fed."

Brooklyn was wiping her eye; the wind probably having

blown some debris into it. McMinn had the same issue, but he was already laying on his stomach. Using kids to fight a guerrilla war? He prayed none of them would be hurt.

"What happens if this is the breeding facility?" Brooklyn asked after a moment.

McMinn's words were cold, spoken through clenched teeth. "No prisoners."

26

Mandy's hands were sore and chapped, old blisters now healing and forming the basis for new calluses. She'd been in the re-education and work camp since the invasion.

"Faster, more efficient. Work better!" The overseer said, snarling the words at her.

She knew soon he was going to make up a bullshit excuse to have a private lesson with her. She'd heard about it from the other young women here. After a while, some went willingly. Their quotas would be lessened, and they were provided with more food and newer clothing, that weren't in tatters or smelled like the dead bodies they'd been stripped from.

"I'm winding these motors as fast as me poor hands can allow, lad," Mandy, or Andy her friends back in Dublin called her.

"You no make quota, three days in row. Today four day. You make quota, or you no eat!" The overseer was a swarthy Chinese man who was nearly as tall as Mandy's chin and was easily one hundred and fifty pounds, half of it lard. He'd been eyeballing her for a week now.

She shuddered at the mental image of his nude body on top of hers, but only showed a rolling of her eyes at the nearly screamed words.

"I always make my quota, you fecking muppet, why don't you go pester the lasses who like short, fat, dumpy men, humping them with their wee peckers?"

His face turned beet red, but Mandy was working hard and winding the electrical motor with the copper wire. She knew she shouldn't have needled the man, but her plan was simple, and she'd finally accumulated enough materials hidden away in her small locker to carry out her escape plan.

The blow was savage. Even being shorter, Overseer Chau snapped her head back with a chop to the chin that left her head spinning.

"You make quota, or else." Mandy focused as her head swam from the blow, but she knew not to fight back, not here.

It was one thing to fight one man, and she knew she was perfectly capable of killing this one by hand, but it was the seventeen guards that rotated through this section of the adhoc factory she'd have to worry about. She'd be shot down in a heartbeat, and being dead was not on her immediate plan of things to do.

"I'll make your fecking quota," Mandy said spitting the blood taste out of her mouth at her feet, turning back to her work.

"Better, or tonight ..." Chau let the words hang there, his eyes locked on her with a hunger that normally would have creeped her out; instead, it filled her with a barely contained rage that her old boyfriend in Tennessee, Jax, would have blamed on her red hair.

"Quit slowing me down. Move your tub so I can wrap these motors," she said, pretending to be cowed.

Overseer Chau leered, then turned and walked away. Inside, Mandy seethed. She'd gotten another pencil, making her small stash of them six now. Waiting until nobody was watching her – even the quality control guy across the aisle from her was bored and talking to his co-worker – did she take the chance and pull her stash out. She'd gotten six small stubs of pencils.

Putting three together, she wrapped a small loop of copper wire over each end, twisting them tight before snipping it off. She repeated this until she had two triangular stacks of pencils about ten centimeters long. Then she pulled about fifty centimeters more of copper wire and dropped it in front of her, along with other scraps. Almost nothing was thrown away and, if questioned, she would claim it was the end of a roll to be put in the recycling.

She was able to quickly catch up and get ahead of her quotas, forming another blister on her left hand, in the pad below her index finger. She made sure that if the overseer of this camp's CTS work and re-education center claimed she'd missed quota again, she'd have witnesses.

"Mandy, what's the rush?" Sarah, the nearly eighteen-year-old who'd been in her left position all week asked, suddenly getting swamped with Mandy's parts.

"I kinna let the swarthy bastard say I never hit me quota," Mandy said, figuring some of the truth wouldn't hurt.

"But you've been hitting it daily. If you didn't, there would be no way I could?" Her words rang true, but Mandy had been suspicious of her since they moved her to take the bolter's job down the assembly line from her.

"It doesn't make any sense to me, but it's not your ass that's on the line," she told Sarah, truthfully. "Unless it really is."

"What do you mean?" Sarah asked, her mouth twitching.

"Yer too slick by far, too well fed. Ye claim yer about to hit eighteen, but you're much too mature for ya age, lass. So, who are you really working for?" Mandy wasn't sure if it was her nature as a red head, or the Irish getting up her blood, because she shouldn't have said that.

A look of anger crossed Sarah's face and she opened and closed her mouth a few times, before shaking her head and rolling her eyes.

27

THE END of shift hadn't been the end of things. Both ladies and lads were led out separate doors and to opposite sides of the compound. The ladies disrobed and showered quickly. Sexual assault wasn't common in the shower rooms, but it had happened. None of the young ladies wanted to be nude in front of their guards any longer than they had to. Each was required to quickly wash in cold water before heading to a thin supper.

Mandy hurried, barely getting wet. She knew Chau would be coming for her tonight. What she'd spirited out of the factory was hid easily in one hand, and none of the birds she was showering with gave two shies, nor cared. Talking was discouraged and most of them had been forced to deal with Chau one way or another. She wondered if the chairman fancied the boys the same way and shuddered at another unfortunate mental image. She quickly dressed in fresh overalls, her loot in her left pocket, before heading to supper.

Nobody talked to Mandy much, though she had long since quit trying to make friends here. Something about her made the ladies either avoid her or made them snarl at her.

She was slightly taller than many of the lasses in her group at 178 centimeters tall, or about five foot ten inches in the complicated American system of measure. Her fiery red hair had a natural loose curl to it, and her mop was usually controlled with a black bandanna, if nothing else to keep it out of her face.

"Is this seat taken?" A boy's question startled her from her thoughts of escape.

"My feet are there, bugger off."

"There's nowhere else to sit." His words were soft, so Mandy rolled her eyes and pulled her legs back in front of her.

Other than the factory work, this was the only time the two sexes were allowed to mingle, and only for an hour. Mandy usually had her food eaten in five minutes and then just relaxed, or soaked her sore, bruised and blistered hands in the cold water of the lavatory.

"Thanks," the tall young man said, sitting down across from her.

She looked up. His head was a tad smallish, his glasses a bit big, but he wasn't staring at her the way other boys usually did. She wasn't on this boy's menu apparently. Maybe he'd be a good buffer, as long as she could get him to stay sitting there. It would be better than the parade of man-boys who thought she'd appreciate their attention. Little gobshites.

"Your accent is … are you from England?"

Mandy dropped her spoon on the tray and looked up. "Are ye fecking kidding me, or are you taking the piss to me, lad?"

"Irish?" He was shifting in his seat uncomfortably.

"Next you're going to call me a Jackeen?" Mandy asked, her blood temperature rising again.

"I… I don't even know what that means. Sorry, I'm Egghead, Egbert. I didn't mean to—"

"Aye Eggy, and I'm Mandy," she said, letting out a sigh and trying to cool down, she didn't want to run this one off, not yet anyway.

Mandy had always looked at American citizens with skepticism. The news back home made the USA sound at one point like it was an armed camp, waiting for a civil war, or to fend off any invasion. What she'd seen while she had been here had been anything but. The fall of the country had come as a surprise to them as much as it had to her. Still, Mandy found the young lad's lack of guile amusing and he was keeping the spot filled so the muppets that usually tried to talk her up would move on.

"Sorry, it's just ... were you born here?" he asked suddenly.

"Oh, you're a bold one," Mandy said grinning and pointed at his plate. "You going to eat those chips?"

"Chips?"

Mandy had been given a mixture of rice, vegetables and fish. The boy across from her though ...

"Hey, those are my fries!" Egghead said as she snatched a few off his plate.

"Not anymore, mate," she said shoving them in her mouth.

The boy didn't look put off; rather, a smile tugged at the corner of his mouth.

"So, what are you in for?" he asked her.

"Being born, what about you?" Mandy asked in return, without pausing to swallow her mouthful.

"Got caught on purpose," he said taking a big bite from his fish as Mandy's jaw dropped open.

"It's not that desperate out there is it?" she asked.

"Judging by the newly formed bruise on the side of your face, arms and what I can see of your neck, you've been beaten?"

She shook her head at the sudden change in subject, "Naw, I take shite from no man or woman. Now why the feck would ye get caught on purpose?" she asked him.

He just smiled and slid his tray to her, "Oh don't worry, I don't plan on being here long."

She watched as he got up and wandered away. Looking at the two trays in front of her, the girl sitting kitty corner reached for the tray. Food rations had been getting shorter and shorter lately. Mandy saw the hand and waited, then lashed out, slapping her on the knuckles with her spoon.

"I'll gob smack the shite out of your fool head you touch my chips again," Mandy said, before dumping the tray on hers, then pushed the empty one back at the girl.

"Bitch," was the reply she got.

Mandy smiled, knowing she'd angered the lass. No matter. Hopefully, tonight she'd be breaking out of here. All she had to do was wait for the perfect opportunity. She ate in a hurry, oblivious to the angry stares of those around her as she devoured two portions of food. She ignored them. Given the opportunity, these lads and lasses would have done the same.

The five-minute bell rang, and the gymnasium-sized room started to empty out. Mandy waited her turn in line with the other ladies, as they would have one more class before their night's sleep. She was only half paying attention, tapping her pocket to feel the coil of wire when she realized her turn to file through would happen and there was double the compliment of guards.

"You, step aside," a short man said pointing to her when she went to pass through, as two of the five guards stepped in front of the doorway, their Type-95 bullpup rifles aimed at her midsection.

Mandy slowly put her hands up. "I take it ya lads aren't here to buy me a pint of the Black Stuff?"

"You come with," the first man said pointing.

He turned, and Mandy followed, seeing in dismay that the two that had leveled rifles at her had turned to follow her, their guns out at the low and ready. Mandy mentally cursed and wondered if the overseer had found her preparations in the cleaning closet.

"Did I do something wrong, or are ya slagging me?"

"I speak English, why can't this American dog?" a man's voice said from behind her in a heavy Chinese accent.

"Because I'm not an American, lad."

The two men behind her started jabbering in Mandarin, their words undecipherable to Mandy as she followed the third. She broke out into a fine sweat as she realized she was being taken to the overseer's office. If this failed, it was going to be her arse, literally. Failure wasn't an option now that she was sure what Chau had planned. What she was counting on was the moment the two of them were alone.

All the slaps, the chops, the rough hands gripping her arms, spinning her; his foul breath breathing down the back of her neck while he creeped on her and tried to look down her shirt. Either it would all end today and she'd be free, or she'd be dead, with the overseer's tendencies making the plan possible. She'd only briefly entertained going to him willingly, getting him more comfortable with her, but it was a brief moment of madness not to be repeated.

"You no American, why here?" the guard in front of her asked.

The two chattering lads behind her paused, waiting for her answer. Mandy decided on honesty again, as the men escorting her were newer and she'd never seen them abuse anybody.

"I was here studying abroad when you lads came in. I was on the lam with my boyfriend actually."

"Engrish?" He asked, barely looking over his shoulder.

"Irish, Northern Ireland. I was an exchange student."

"You look too old to exchange study," a man behind her said.

They had walked back into the factory portion, where a night shift of young men was working. These were people who could come and go, being trusted party members of the CTS or sympathizers. Many eyes paused their work to admire the red headed beauty being led down the aisleway. Mandy hated the attention and hated wolf whistles more than anything she could imagine, but this lot knew she wasn't being paraded through the factory for their benefit.

"Aye, it was my senior year, then I was headed to the Uni," Mandy told him.

They walked until Mandy could see the metal steps on the back wall that led up to a mezzanine level, where the Overseer had an office walled off. The rumor was that he slept up there. Mandy had only heard about it second and third hand, but the sight of him opening his door, looking down at her and smiling – that look chilled her, making her arms break out in goosebumps.

It was that moment that the guard in front looked over at her. "I sorry, miss. I do what overseer tells me. No choice."

"Don't let it worry you, lad. You fellows going inside with me?" Mandy asked as they all started up the stairs.

"No. Orders to wait here," he said stopping outside the door.

The two behind her that had been jabbering in Mandarin had gone silent as she reached the mezzanine landing. The office itself looked to have been stick constructed with metal sheeting covering the walls. The floors outside of it were gridwork metal. She glanced a look down and almost went dizzy at the twenty feet of empty space and parts for the factory directly below her. If things went wrong and she had to, it was enough of a fall to ... she shook her head and stood up straight. She had to remind herself not to touch her pocket, assuring herself that her surprise was still hidden.

"Please," the nice guard said, opening the door for her.

Surprised by his manners and kind tone, she stepped inside.

28

"Please, sit," Overseer Chau said, then looked at his guard who had remained at the door and jerked his head to the side, indicating he wanted him to leave.

Mandy looked around. She was sitting on the edge of an overstuffed couch across from a desk Chau was sitting behind. His chair must have been on the highest elevation, because he was at eye level with Mandy. The office on the inside was wood paneled with papers and certificates put on the wall in a language Mandy had no idea what it was but suspected a Chinese dialect.

"Here we are," Chau said formally.

She slid her hand into her pocket and let her fingers curl around one bundle of pencil stubs. She could feel the lightly braided copper wire. If one strand broke, there were two more. Her only worry was that it was too stiff to use properly when the time came. She didn't think so, but the worry was still there.

"I made my production, Overseer," Mandy said, remembering to use his title and not to call him a muppet again.

"No, still behind. We talk; you want to eat, you make more parts. Lots."

"I can't go any faster than I am, you think I'm acting the maggot?" Mandy asked, biting back a more cutting retort, "And what of everyone downline from me? If I am not hitting production, they cannot themselves. Eh?"

"I don't think you understand how this works," he said in surprisingly clear English.

That made her sit up straight. He could speak perfect English without an accent? He was holding back that tidbit. If he was holding that back, what else was he hiding? Mandy chanced a glance out the door's window, seeing the guards had retreated down the mezzanine, probably not wanting to listen to her rape. She almost wondered if she called for help, would the lead guard come to her aid? She doubted it.

"I know exactly how this works, you fecking miscreant," Mandy hissed. "Ya won't be getting me out of my pants over some fake cooked up paperwork. I'm not selling my arse so cheap."

Overseer Chau's eyebrows went up and he stroked the thin beard on his chin.

"Who said I wanted your arse?" he said mimicking her accent.

Mandy stood up, rolling her shoulders, getting on the balls of her feet.

"Ah, a fighter, good. I like breaking you American sluts. When I'm done with you, you'll beg for it. You'll be willing and even eager."

"For a pecker the size of my wee little finger?" she asked, putting a mocking note in her voice and holding her hand up, showing him her small hand, pinky extended.

The taunt worked. Chau turned red, high in his cheeks and ears.

"It is no matter," he said standing, starting to come

around the desk. "The guards know you will be difficult. I have standing orders to take you to either the hospital ward or isolation depending on your condition after I'm done with you."

"You're a disgusting boyo, not worth the spit of a slug. You disgust me. You make buzzards puke."

He moved fast, closing the distance. Mandy saw the movement and had time to pull the garrote out of her pocket. Chau was watching her face and missed her movement, thinking she was turning for the door. She wasn't doing any of that, but he swung so fast she didn't see the blow coming until it was too late to dodge. She turned her head slightly, taking a punch to the side of the head.

Despite being taller than him and nearly the same weight as the short tub of shite, the blow rocked Mandy. She bounced off the couch, her back smacking into the left wall the couch had rested on next to the door. Chau was still looking at her eyes, drinking in the look of pain and the brief look of real fear that washed over her face. Seeing her rocked, he straddled her knees, pushed her right hand back and tore at the top of her overalls.

It was the opening Mandy had been waiting for. She shook the garrote out with her left hand and swung it. The wire was stiff, but still had the partial shape of the coil to help it out. It wrapped around his neck as he was pulling at the front of her bra. He paused for a second as Mandy pistoned her knee upwards, one leg no longer trapped. She caught him by surprise and as he started expelling air, she brought her other hand around and grabbed the loose end of the garrote and pulled it across his throat. Tight.

Suddenly realizing what was going on, his hands had gone to his throat, pulling at the wire. Mandy had planned on doing this from behind him if at all possible, but she didn't have much of a choice now. He clawed at her hands until she took a chance and head butted him. The blow dazed both of them, but she was able to make enough room between them that he pulled his head back.

Desperation filled Chau's face, and he threw a quick and sloppy right-hand punch. Mandy tried to dodge but holding the garrot with both hands she didn't have anywhere to go. The blow caught her right in the nose, immediately sending a spray of blood. She screamed, her voice high-pitched. She didn't have to pretend that it hurt – it really did hurt. That momentary lapse of attention gave Chau a chance to grab her right wrist with both of his hands and start pulling. Rivulets of blood started running down the side of his neck as the copper wire bit into his flesh.

"Not bloody likely, you fecking muppet," Mandy snarled, spraying his face with the blood that was running across her lips.

She used her knee as a piston once again and when it connected, Chau's face went white with pain. The half a breath he had gotten when he had pulled her wrist was immediately cut off. Without thinking, Chau put both hands to his throat and tried pulling the wire away again. Mandy had been ready for this and started twisting the wire hand over hand. Chau's right hand was trapped at the base of his throat, but Mandy kept twisting and tying, giving him no room to pull the garrot free.

"You will not be touching another lass, nor another lass's arse, you piece a shite," Mandy told him as she watched his movements start to slow.

She watched as his eyes bugged out and then shoved him as hard as she could with her open palms. He started slumping and gravity was working against Mandy. She wasn't able to push him backwards, so she slid to her right, able to leverage him just enough so that he fell face forward, his head hitting the wall.

"No, I don't want to, you can't make me!" Mandy started screaming in a high-pitched voice as she walked around the office, saying it for the benefit of the guards if they had stayed where they were supposed to be.

She had to work fast and went to the only other door in the room which was behind his desk. She walked back there and opened it up. Filing cabinets lined two of the four walls, but the other two were taken up by a large king-sized bed, a small dresser, and a mini fridge. She noted there was no bathroom up here in his quarters, and wondered if the rumors were true, that he never bathed. He sure smelled like he never did.

Mandy let out another high-pitched scream and started kicking and stomping at the floor. What she was really doing though, was opening up the file cabinets and looking through them. They all appeared to be dossiers, including pictures. In the third file cabinet from the right she found her file. When she opened it up it had her picture, their estimated age of her, which was wrong, and what they knew about her health history.

She scanned through it and noted they also had her blood type and ancestry marked down. That puzzled her and worried her a little bit at the same time. There was a check mark about fertility. This was stranger and stranger. Mandy saw that they were screening men and women here for something medical but didn't know what.

She went to another filing cabinet, one that had the lock popped out on the front. She pulled the first drawer open and sitting right on top were two files that had not been properly put away. They were sitting on top of everything else in the drawer. Mandy could see that one of them was not in alphabetical order like the other files.

"Egbert," she said, as she opened the file, seeing his name in black felt marker.

Sure enough, it had a picture of a bird in there but much of the data in the file was still blank or missing. There was a pink sticky note on the front of the folder that she ignored at first. She flipped it back closed and read the note: *connection to Archie.*

"Archie?" Mandy said, then let out another high-pitched scream and started pretending to beg and repeat no, over and over and over.

She opened the other file that had been placed on top and saw right away what it was. Archie was a veteran that the CTS had captured and had been believed to have been executed. There was a new note in the file that said, despite photographic evidence, Archie had survived the gunshot to the head. He had been linked to a resistance movement.

She quickly scanned through the notes they had on this resistance movement – some guy name McMinn, along with a list of other names, Egbert being one of them.

"So ya got caught on purpose, ay buddy?" she asked no one. "Looks like these blokes might've been hip to you from the start."

Dark red drops started falling on the files. With a start, Mandy realized that she'd been dripping blood all over the place. She was pretty sure her nose was broken but it'd started off as a gush and had slowed rapidly. To make this ruse work she would need to keep the guards out of here long enough to go to the hospital ward. She had a plan if they took her to the isolation/lockup instead, but the hospital ward put her right next to the supply closet she'd stored her stuff in.

She hurried into the other room and put her hands under Chau's armpits and slowly dragged him off the couch. His body hitting the floor had one of the guards look up just as Mandy noticed his movement from outside the door. She crouched down and started yanking him as hard as she could toward the back door.

"Overseer Chau?" a guard's voice rang out behind the steel door, just as Mandy slammed the door behind her and the overseer's corpse.

"No, I don't want to, it hurts, it hurts!" she screamed, as she used all of her core body strength to push the overseer onto the bed.

She screamed again as there was a knocking at the steel door in the outer office. She hoped she was convincing enough, otherwise they might beat her to death before she had a chance to make her escape. What the guards would do in the next thirty seconds might change the outcome of her entire plan.

There was a lot riding on this. She pulled the blankets over the overseer, and then looked down to see her overalls covered in blood, the top ripped open, her black bra and chest covered in her own blood. She unzipped her overalls down to near her waistline and made sure the blood was smeared all over her hands, her face, her chest, and her stomach.

She heard the outer office door burst open and two voices call out in Chinese. She opened the door to the office and slid out slamming the file room/bedroom door behind her. She screamed as if she was in fear and ran to the first guard that had been kind to her while leaving her up here.

"No more, no more, no more! Please?" she asked, falling to her knees in front of him as if in supplication.

"How bad you hurt?" The kind guard asked her, offering an arm to help her stand up.

"My nose doesn't hurt as bad as ..." She let the words trail off and then shot a long glance at the closed door where the overseer's body was tucked in neatly.

One of the guards that had been behind her joined the nice guard in the doorway and smiled, poking him in the ribs.

The nice guard kind of shoved him back, either making more room or showing his disgust.

"You come, we will take you to doctor. They fix nose. They give you ... after morning pill. Morning after ... whatever."

Mandy didn't say anything as the nice guard pushed past the other two, closing the office door behind them. They led her back down the mezzanine staircase toward the factory floor. Men would look up as they walked through, but seeing her condition and her attempts to hold her bloodstained overalls closed, they quickly looked away.

She hadn't planned on getting hurt or busted up at all, but if she had the chance, she was going to let the doctor set her nose. Then the real shenanigans could begin. The kind guard looked back to make sure she was following close, and she gave him a shy grin. The sight of her bloodied teeth made him shudder and he turned back around, walking a little bit faster, trying not to run. Her plan was working. So far, so good.

29

Mandy didn't see the doctor right away, but she was given two generic pain pills and another one she figured was their birth control. She rinsed her mouth out from the drinking fountain, making sure there was no blood, then swallowed the pills, knowing she didn't need the Plan B pill, but taking it anyway. Things in the back were unusually busy with people running in and out of the room.

The front of the hospital ward was heavily guarded, but she was mostly alone in her room. She'd left the front of her overalls open as if they'd been ripped from her, with her blood drying to a crust on her chest and stomach. She'd wiped up her face as much as she could after swallowing the pills, but without a bathroom mirror she didn't know how bad it looked.

"Mandy O'Hanson," a woman's voice called before knocking on the door and entering the small room Mandy had been put in to wait.

She understood why they didn't want to keep her in public, even though she wasn't very hurt to begin with. She looked exactly like what she wanted to look, a survivor of a sexual assault. She was using everyone's squeamishness to divert attention and hopefully allow her a chance to make it to the woman's restroom alone.

"Aye, that's me." Her words were quiet, but she made herself sound more pained and less confident than she actually was.

A woman in her mid-forties came in, her hair pulled up into a severe-looking bun. Her gray hair seemed to be pinned in place with two sharpened pencils, which Mandy noted as a potential sharp object to acquire and use if necessary. She was wearing a white doctor's coat, and beneath that a set of blue scrubs. She had those rubberized orthopedic shoes that walking billboards for abstinence showed.

"Mandy, it says here you're almost nineteen years old. Exchange student from Ireland, originally from the Dublin area. You have all the required immunizations that were up-to-date until …" The woman broke off her words and looked at Mandy, her features American, then she looked in the direction the guards were standing and scowled, "and you're here today because some asshole broke your nose and I see they've already given you the Plan B pill."

"Aye, the overseer, the sorry bastard, though he'd manufactured a reason to get him a piece of me arse," Mandy said coldly, wondering why this lady was working with the Chinese when she clearly hated them.

"Are you in any pain?" she asked. "I can help, but they won't let me prescribe – "

"How many lasses have you treated? How many rapes do you allow to happen under your roof, and how many aborted babies do ye kill on average?"

The Irish was rising in Mandy again, and she wasn't very happy. Truth was the only thing that hurt was her nose, but to see someone semi-willingly working with the Chinese and not fighting back? That made her all kinds of pissed off, and when Mandy O'Hanson got pissed off people understood why redheads had a fierce reputation.

The doctor had a name tag that said *Fikes* on her white lab coat. Mandy took in the rest of her features. She looked like she'd once been slender but now gentle curves filled out her frame. Then she did a double-take – the doctor was not nearly as old as Mandy had originally thought; rather she was working under tremendous strain.

"I have absolutely no choice in the matter," she said, tears threatening to spill down her cheeks. "They have my husband and my daughter locked up here. I'm good at healing people, even if I'm doing it after the monsters hurt the innocent. Can you blame me for trying to do my best for you?"

"I just ..." Mandy's anger fizzled at that moment, and she realize the doctor was right. She was working here of her own free will, but she was doing everything she could to counter the mess the Chinese had brought to the American shores.

"I'm sorry, Doc," Mandy said rubbing the bridge of her nose where she felt a large bloodied knot. "I'm angry at the whole fucking world right now and my nose is hurting." She leaned forward and in a softer tone said, "And I'm hoping to get me arse out of this joint soon. I don't suppose you all wouldn't love to do the same?"

Dr. Fikes walked closer to Mandy and put her right hand on the young woman's face, then she put her left hand on the other side, cradling her face and pulled her closer. In a quiet voice the doctor said, "Don't we all?" Then her thumbs pushed to the sides of Mandy's nose and pulled.

A bolt of pain shot through Mandy's head, and then she jerked out of the doctor's reach. New drips of blood fell down her front, but Mandy had felt the moment her nose had been set straight. It was not something she bloody likely ever wanted to feel again. She held one hand under her nose while Dr. Fikes reached into her lab coat pocket and tore open some gauze. She handed the gauze to Mandy and left the room.

Mandy wondered if she'd said too much, but Dr. Fikes was back a moment later with a handful of supplies. The first thing she did was punch a chemical ice pack, knead it, and hand it over to Mandy. Pinching her nose with the gauze, Mandy put the ice pack over her face.

"Your nose set pretty easy, there's a possibility you'll have a small bump or a scar where it broke, but without proper supplies it's the best I can do." Then she leaned in with a quieter voice again, "and if you have some sort of plan, keep it to yourself. You can trust me but some of my nurses are collaborators, just like some of the people that work on the floor in the factory."

Mandy pulled the ice pack back to study her and nodded. "I've had to learn quick who I can trust and who isn't worth the shite the Lord scraped off his shoes. If you could tape me up and then let me use the bathroom, I'll be out of your hair superfast."

"Part of the Ray protocol the Chinese have forced on us is to always have a guard nearby when someone is using the restroom. I don't let them come inside the bathroom because there's no point. There are no windows; one door in and one door out. You can have your privacy if you need to cry. But I can't have you doing anything stupid in there."

"Do something stupid? Do you think I'm gonna try to off myself like some crying fucking violet?" Mandy asked her with a little laugh at the end.

Dr. Fikes was ready and taped her nose and advised her to put the cold pack back on top. Mandy held it there barely able to see the short doctor over it.

"You know, cut your wrists, jump out a window, hang

yourself, all that stuff's been tried before, and the guards know to look for it."

"I know what you fucking mean," Mandy said testily. "I'm not a suicide case. I just want to wash my arse. I told you, I'm getting out of here."

"And how are you doing that?" the doctor asked her.

"I've a feeling all hell's about to break loose, so if I were you I would be ready when the time comes."

Dr. Fikes shook her head and reached in her pocket and pulled out a small, plain white pill bottle. She handed it to Mandy and walked out of the room letting the door swing closed behind her with a bang.

"Bloody hell, she's either the bravest woman in here, or a complete nutter."

The door banged open and a Chinese guard was there, the nice one from earlier. Mandy quickly tried to cover herself with her overalls, but he was already turning away, his face red.

"Doctor say you need chaperone. I am ... it was unfortunate ... I offered to do it myself in case other guard not so kind."

Mandy pulled her overalls closed as much as she could with one hand and stood up. She was half a head taller than the guard and when she tried to meet his eyes, he turned his face.

"You dunna have to be ashamed for me, lad," she said softly, realizing he was only a handful of years older. "I'm still alive and ye've not done nothing to impinge upon your own honor. Ye've been kindest of all, and I appreciate your offer to be the chaperone."

She did, but she also felt bad, because it was almost time to make her escape and she was worried that if she failed, he'd be blamed and punished. He was the only decent Chinese guard she'd run across to date. He nodded at her words and motioned with his hand for her to follow him before turning and holding the door open with his other hand behind him.

Mandy followed, and when she pushed the door with her shoulder, he let it go. She dumped the ice pack into the first bin she saw. It would have to be enough, and she prayed it was. She knew she was going to have two black eyes, but she also worried about one of them swelling shut. So far it hadn't happened, but the night was early, and the overseer's body hadn't been found yet.

"If you wait, I have washcloth and new cover," he said, pointing to her overalls, "coming from laundry. You wash up, put on clean clothes. Use bathroom first, then come back here and I have things ready."

Mandy was surprised at that and nodded. She'd go along with it until she had clean overalls. She didn't want to make a spectacle of herself being blood-stained, but sometimes the Lord provided, and he was smiling down upon her right now. She promised herself she was parking her arse in the next bloody Catholic church she saw when she got out of this bolloxed shit box of an institution.

"Where's the loo?" she asked, following him.

"Through," he replied, still leading.

She followed him through a doorway where there had been a mass of people coming in and out earlier. It was a triage area, with four beds lined up in a hallway section beyond the door. One of them held a figure in bloodied sheets, moaning softly. Mandy hoped it wasn't another lass, coming from having the worst moment of her life. Then the sheet moved, and she let out a gasp, recognizing the boy's face.

"Wait," Mandy called to her guard. "Eggy, is that you?" she asked, walking to the bed.

"Mandy?" he replied quietly.

"Aye, lad. What are ye doing in here? Fighting the world?"

"Sort of," he said, looking at the guard warily. "Getting caught on purpose might not have been such a good idea after all," he added, still eying the guard. "I think they busted a few teeth out and my ribs feel bruised. Are you okay?" he asked her, taking in the blood-stained clothing and puffy face.

"Sort of," she shot back at him, admiring how the beating he'd taken that had put him in a hospital bed hadn't broken his spirit. "The fecking overseer busted me nose."

"She need go now," the nice guard told him and gently pulled on Mandy's arm. She let him do it, knowing she could have broken his arm in three places before he had a chance to react or call out an alarm. Knowing that and not acting was making her twitchy.

"Let me talk to the lad a moment more, will ye? I've taken a shine to this one and ... I have things to tell him."

She batted her eyelashes, but not to flirt, but in what she hoped looked like mock shame. It worked, and he gave her a quick nod, then backed up to the doorway. Mandy put her hands together and gave him a mock bow and smile, then turned back to Egghead.

"So, you've taken a shine to me, eh? Did the overseer ... did he ... take advantage of you? Are you okay?"

The words were a vocal diarrhea of sorts, and she suddenly saw that he was absolutely terrified. It was infectious; either that, or Mandy was starting to think about the cooling body of Chau upstairs.

"Sort of. You're an interesting lad. No, the overseer just busted me nose. I'll be okay, but he won't be," she said smiling.

"He won't be ..." When the realization hit, it was like watching a light bulb turn on behind his eyes and Mandy nodded to him when he got it.

"So, I won't be here long, lad, and there's something you should know. They know all about you, some guy named Archie and McMinn and a ragtag army of kids. Bloody wolverines or some shite like that. How bad are you really hurt?"

The last was whispered, as Mandy leaned forward so they were almost face to face. She looked back and saw the guard watching. He looked away quickly.

"I hurt, but not as bad as I make it seem," he admitted. "Why? How soon are things going to get crazy?"

"I'm going to the loo. When you hear the gates of hell kicked in, you make yourself scarce, and stay away from the smoke and fire. I have a feeling they're going to have to let the people outside to the gates before long. I just pray nobody is hurt."

"What are you going to do?" Eggy asked.

She brushed aside the hair on his forehead and leaned down, pressing her lips against it in what she hoped would be taken as a gesture of affection by the watching guard, and now nurse who had joined him in the doorway, their brows furrowed as she whispered to him.

"I'm going to blow the fecking bastards into bloody bits."

"You're IRA, aren't you?" Eggy asked suddenly.

"No, ya silly boyo. I watched too much YouTube growing up!" She snickered and stood.

Egghead touched his forehead where her lips had made contact. His face was turning red around the purple areas. Mandy gave him a little wave and then nodded her head to the nice guard. He came forward.

"Now I gotta go before I piss myself," she said to both.

The guard pointed at a door with his finger, his lips pinched at her vulgarity. She grinned and followed him as he opened it, showing a single stall bathroom, a sink hanging off the wall, with a heavy-duty toilet against the adjoining wall, and a stainless-steel grab bar on the left side of the porcelain throne.

"Thank ya mate, I think I got it here," she told him, closing the door.

"No locking," the guard called back.

"Not bloody likely," Mandy whispered to the door.

30

SHE IMMEDIATELY TURNED on the water and turned the lock slowly until she heard it click. She hoped the water would be enough to mask the sound, but she doubted the guard would be outside the door in case she was doing something like dropping a load, let alone piss loudly. Mandy almost snickered. That guard was the best of the lot, but he seemed very naïve or very, very shy. She hoped it was shy. She turned the water off, then walked over to the toilet. Everything in this room was white: the fecking walls, the tile on the floor and the drop ceiling with its white fecking gridwork.

Mandy stood on the toilet, then put one foot up on the grab bar, leveraging herself high enough to push one of the ceiling tiles up. She slid it aside and boosted herself up on the partitioning wall. She'd already mapped this and knew she'd had the luck of the Irish. That had made her grin like none other. She didn't have far to crawl through the utility access points. She replaced the ceiling tile and lifted the tile in the adjoining space and tossed it aside. She wouldn't be coming back this way.

The strong smell of chemicals wafted to her as she

lowered herself halfway through the opening. It made her smile. She made sure to grab the box on top of the wall divider before getting all the way down. Using the utility closet shelf as a ladder, she made it to the floor soundlessly. That's when Mandy cracked open the box. Inside she'd smuggled a few things, mostly the metal containers and discarded cans from the mess hall that she'd rinsed out. It wasn't as reactive when she had been mixing and experimenting.

"If this works, ya little boyos are going to get you a big surprise," she said, her grin almost a rictus of pain from her broken nose.

"Where she go?" she heard somebody yelling in the distance.

"Time to make the donuts, lads," Mandy said, opening the door.

She'd gone to another wing of the entire place by just crawling a few feet across another wall. She'd discovered the dead space that the utilities and heating and cooling systems had occupied above the drop ceiling and had been squirreling supplies away, and then she'd made the TATP.

It's right dangerous stuff, but the Chinese were shipping everything over and it must have been cheaper to ship the concentrated hydrogen peroxide rather than the diluted stuff. She'd found a lot of it in the cleaning closet of all places, but did people clean with that shite? Mandy didn't know, she hoped to figure life out someday, when she wasn't locked up.

"I hope this bloody works." She pulled a cloth satchel out of her metallic box and packed the five containers she'd prepped and wrapped with rags, so they didn't knock together, then opened the door.

Pounding feet had her looking to the right, seeing guards running toward the corner where the hospital wing was separated from the rest of the area. She was between the manufacturing plant and the public restrooms. She grinned. It wouldn't take long to find where she'd gone and how she got out. She had to move fast. Communications was her first order of business. She wanted it cut off if at all possible, but first she had to do something right here.

"Hey, you!" A shout had her turning to look back to her right. Two guards were running at her.

"Hope this works," she said putting a can down and, using a Bic lighter she'd stashed, lighting the shoelace she'd spent hours cutting in half and twisting.

It started burning and Mandy took off running toward the manufacturing side.

"Stop, we shoot!" Another voice yelled from behind her.

Mandy was running full stride, her long legs giving her an enormous advantage over the shorter, and consequently shorter legged, pursuers. She knew that they weren't joking though, they would shoot. No matter how fast she could run, she couldn't outrun their AK's. She hit the polished tile, sliding like a runner would in baseball just as two things happened. The wall next to her erupted from a gunshot, followed half a second later by a small roaring explosion.

She glanced back seeing the hallway filled with smoke, chunks of pink and red things splattering as gravity finally took over, or they dripped off the ceiling.

"Good, now we know it works," she said with a grin.

Regaining her feet, Mandy almost flinched as the sirens went off and the sprinklers doused the entire hallway with water.

"Oh shit, I dinna think o' that," Mandy cursed herself, now running and trying not to fall across the slick surface of the tile.

Her plan was to gain the door just inside the manufacturing plant, run down that hallway to the communications room, disable it with one of her bombs, and then out the set of double doors that one of the guards had shown her when she'd first moved from janitorial to the production floor. He had ideas of romance, but when she spurned his advances, she was reassigned.

She knew that it led to the fuel depot outside. If she put one of her fuses there, she might blow half the north fence out, as well as the wall. She also might fry herself to a crisp, but she'd promised herself that she'd get out no matter what.

"What's going on?" a man in coveralls asked, screaming from the doorway to the manufacturing side, joined a second later by a guard looking around his shoulder.

"Some arse wipes blew something up down by the hospital!" Mandy yelled, running right at them. "The chem closet is going to blow!"

They stood there staring at her. Mandy's feet were making a slapping sound, and she felt a breeze. She looked down to see her blood covered chest and stomach once again, though the water was washing the red away. Feck, she didn't change and had hardly wiped herself up. The man started to run but the guard shouted something at him as he was yanked back in the doors by multiple arms.

Mandy hadn't entirely lied, she knew what was in that closet, but she wasn't running from an explosion, she was running from two chemicals mixing together. She was pretty sure the explosion had knocked over the bleach she'd put in a paint can with a loose lid. It was mixing with another can of ammonia. The smell would hit soon if it had happened, creating a noxious cloud that would cut off pursuers from that side of the building, cutting down the guards by two thirds.

"Out of my way!" Mandy yelled as three guards' faces filled the doorway, their words lost over the wailing of the siren and the low roar of the sprinklers dumping water.

At the last second, one of them recognized her and brought his rifle up. Not able to stop, Mandy once again decided to go low in a baseball slide, holding the cloth bag to her stomach. Now that the tiled floor was slick from water, she had a lot more momentum going. Ten feet. Five. A gun tracked her, and a shot rang out just as her lifted leg impacted the shooters knee. She heard a sickening snap as the guard fell, his screams drowning out the din of noise from the alarms.

She bounded to her feet, but shoes still wet, she slipped. One of the three guards tried to make a grab for her, but she pulled back at the last second and snapped a kick out, catching him high in the ribs. The blow pushed him into the other guard, knocking both of them to the ground next to the man rolling around, holding his leg to his stomach.

"What's going on?" the man who'd been pulled back in screamed, pulling on Mandy's shoulder.

The fabric of her open overalls had more give than he expected, and when Mandy spun, he also wasn't expecting the solid right-hand chop that took him in the side of the throat. He made a quick choking sound, letting go, hands going to his waist as he bent over to breathe.

"Sorry, bubba boyo," she said to him, breathlessly. "Didn't know who ye was at first. Pro tip, don't grab a lass unless she gives you permission, got it?"

He fell to the ground as well, on all fours, finally taking in big deep gasping breaths. Mandy was aware of the volatile substances in the bag, the slide, and the fighting. It all could have been enough to blow her to hell and back, but she'd been generous with the padding and her prayers were heard that she hadn't been hit with—

"Smell?" One of the guards barked, regaining his feet and pulling at his partner, coughing.

Mandy ran. They could follow her, they could shoot her, but suddenly the acrid smell of chemicals was almost overpowering. She had to hurry, or her window of opportunity would close. She ran for all she was worth, her right hand cradling the satchel, the lighter in her other hand. The communications room materialized and she almost slid past it. She looked inside and saw a panicked guard. She burst in the door.

"Get out! Somebody's attacking us with chemical weapons! We must flee!"

"What? How you get here? You no supposed—"

"The bloody arseholes down the hallway sent me. We must evacuate, so hurry!"

She didn't want to hurt him if she didn't have to but was more than willing to give this a shot before she resorted to violence again. Her hand was sore and she didn't want to bust herself up fighting everyone, wearing herself out, when what she really should be doing was running.

"You come," he said getting to his feet and motioning to her.

"Ye lead," she panted out to him.

That's when he saw the cloth sack and the lighter in her hand. His panicked face then took in Mandy's gaze. When he went for the radio, she was already in motion. He'd knelt to press the button to talk, to alert the whole fecking facility. Mandy had other plans. Her foot shot out, kicking him in the elbow, throwing his entire arm upwards. She held the bag tight and shot out her leg again as he started to yell, her foot impacting with his temple. He dropped like the sack of shit he was.

Mandy looked around, and seeing no one else, dragged him backwards by his shoulders outside into the hallway. If the poison gas got to him, she didn't mind. None of the Chinese here deserved any better, and unless those in the manufacturing side got trapped by something stupid, they should be running outside the other set of doors on the opposite side of the property any second now.

Mandy turned the deadbolts on the big doors, then looked around the communications room. She went to the radio and yanked the handset out, the cords ripping free. She thought about picking up the chair and smashing it, but then looked back at the file cabinets and what she saw on top of it. An old iPod, really old.

"Now the bastard's got my curiosity piqued," Mandy muttered and snatched it up.

She started scrolling through the songs, seeing it had probably belonged to a lady before it was confiscated by the guards here. It was a lot of girl bands, but one in particular stuck out to her, and she was glad she hadn't damaged the PA system yet.

"Patti, you'd love this song, girl," she muttered, remembering a dear friend from Ireland. She ran to the controls.

The microphone jack plugged into the iPod and she hit play and repeat. *In This Moment* boomed, as the opening to the song, *Blood*s blared.

"This is some good music to open the dance, don't ye think?" she called to the doorway she'd taken the guard out through.

Mandy's gaze then went to the double doors. Outside. Freedom. Almost. Then the lyrics got heavy, the words of the song booming all over the entire facility. Goosebumps covered Mandy's arms as she pushed through the double doors and went outside.

It was dark now, and although she had the harsh chemical smell of the chlorine gas in her nose, she could also smell something burning, and saw a streamer of smoke along the edge of the building. Grinning, she looked straight ahead to the motor pool. Men were running and in half a heartbeat, she saw what looked like a short-bus version of a firetruck headed in the direction of the smoke.

"Almost too easy—"

Gunfire raked the building near her, and a spotlight came on, pinning her in place. The shots had been warning shots. She slid to a stop and put her arms up.

"Mandy, go!" She recognized that voice and took off at a sprint.

There were three large tanks above the ground, near a couple of trucks. She headed that way until a figure stood up, making her slide to a stop, almost pitching her ass over teakettle.

"Mandy, over here!" Egbert screamed, holding his side, where he'd broken his ribs.

"You muppet!" she yelled back as the gunfire went silent. "What the bloody hell are you doing?"

"My friends are here," he said, grinning. "They took care of the guys shooting at you. They're also about to blow the fence."

"Well then, let's give them a bloody hand," Mandy said pulling out a soup can, then putting the entire bag down under the fuel tanks.

"What are ..."

"It's TATP. It's still sorta wet, so it's not quite as dangerous as it could be. Now I'm going to light this fecking satchel and you run like the devil's nipping at your girly bits."

"Girly bits?"

Mandy chuckled as she lit the fuse, knowing the explosion or burning cloth bag would ignite the rest of the bombs. Egghead looked at her in a strange light, then realized what she'd done. She stood, yanking his shoulder, almost pulling him off his feet.

"Which way do we go?" he screamed.

Mandy was already moving. The skinny, lanky man-child wasn't moving fast enough from being injured, and being a fit lass, she put the bomb in his hand and then took him in a fireman's carry. Gunfire peppered the ground, though she wasn't sure who was shooting at whom. When she'd mentally counted to eight ... nine ... ten ... she dropped to the ground, rolling on top of a screaming Egghead behind a parked military vehicle of some sort, opening her mouth, trying to tell him to do the same while covering him and the last bomb.

The explosion earlier was nothing in comparison to the thunderous boom behind her. The ground seemed to tremble, then open up. Glass shattered for half a mile. An angry avenging god had dropped the hammer. A dozen different anecdotes for the sound went through her head, but the one thing she could say without a doubt – it was the biggest sound ever.

Feeling like all the air had been sucked out of her lungs, Mandy looked around. Something flaming crashed into the armored vehicle they had slid behind. A second set of explosions rocked the night, though Mandy and Egghead were deafened from being so close to the first set. Mandy rolled off Egbert, pulling the bomb out of his hands, before trying to pull him to his feet.

"Look, there they are!" Egghead yelled, but she was reading his lips.

She followed his hand as dozens of figures rushed through the breach in the fence. Two of them broke off, pointing at Mandy and Egbert, who was trying to wave them down with the arm that wasn't holding the muppet's guts in from his busted ribs.

"Who are they?" Mandy hollered, not knowing if he could hear her or not.

"My friends. My family," he told her, though this time she could hear him.

Screams from the work camp were almost nonstop now, mostly shouting to coordinate firefighting efforts in two languages. Gunfire rang out from all around the fence. Mandy pulled Eggy with her toward the breach, but he yanked his hand back as a lass with dark glasses and a tall thin man in camo clothing, a dog following along behind them, approached. All were heavily armed, right out of a *Soldier of Fortune* magazine: side arms, what looked like the same rifles the Chinese had been using ...

"How bad are you hurt?" the man said without pause to Egbert.

"Busted ribs," he replied, then they all hit the ground as rounds started hitting over their head. "Who's your friends?" he screamed to the two newcomers.

"Locals who have family locked up in here. Sorry it took us so long," the pale skinned woman said, brushing the side of his face. "You've got blood coming out of your ears."

They were now all prone behind the armored vehicle, an APC of sorts as gunfire rang out around them. Mandy crawled on her hands and knees as she saw civilians running through the fencing, some coming, some going. Chinese soldiers were trying to stop a massive escape from happening, trying to fight a fire, and fighting off the people who were assisting in the escape all at the same time.

"There's not enough of the CTS to put up much of a fight," the man said rising to his knees and firing his rifle in neat sounding three round bursts.

"There's enough of the bloody fecking bastards to take the piss right out of my plans," Mandy snarked back at him, ducking as bullets rang out on the bumper she was trying to look around. "Shit," she swore.

She then remembered the bomb in her right hand and grinned. She could see the pocket of CTS firing from behind the burning hulk of a transport truck. That's when she realized her left hand was empty.

"What are you looking for?" The pale woman in dark glasses asked her.

"I need a lighter," she said, patting the pockets of her overalls.

The man who'd been firing pulled something out of a breast pouch in his vest and tossed it to her. A Zippo. Mandy caught it on the fly and lit the fuse. The flame flickered but caught. Her hands shook as she put the fuse and flame together.

"Cover me!" she screamed.

Both the man and pale woman stood and started firing.

Mandy had learned to love American softball while she was an exchange student. She'd been a top athlete and had scholarships awaiting her at the Uni if she ever got out of the country. Running, pole vaulting – her parents had even hoped one day she might have been interested in the Olympics of all the fecking bloody ridiculous things. The running she did willingly, but her entire life, she had fallen in love with the martial arts and had been practicing Krav Maga since middle school. Still, the softball bug had bit her hard, and she'd been an excellent pitcher.

She wound up and tossed the burning can underhanded, going more for accuracy than speed. The flame of the can made it easy for her to track its progress in the dark. She stayed up half a second too long and when the ground erupted all around, something hot and sharp cut into her side before she dropped to the ground. She rubbed her cheek, her hand coming back with a red smear as another explosion rocked the night and the gunfire coming at them ceased.

"You got them!" the man said, his gun falling silent.

Mandy wanted to run, but suddenly her limbs felt like jelly, her inner bits wobbly and nauseous. She leaned against the APC's big tire and listened as the explosions and gunfire tapered off to nothing. She watched as civilians fled the area around them, some running all the way around the fence, calling names she didn't know.

"How bad are you hit?" Egghead asked, pulling something from his pocket and holding it against Mandy's cheek.

"I'm not hit!" she shot back.

"Cut from a ricochet," the man told Eggy.

"Well shit, my Ma and Pa always said Americans were a funny lot, liked to worry me to death about getting shot and now ..."

They shook their heads, Egghead rolling his eyes.

"You three stay here. I've got to link up with the local resistance and I'll have the medic that came in yesterday come check on you all. It sounds like things here are wrapping up."

Mandy looked at the man as he tapped his ear. An earpiece was connected to a clip on the vest. He must have been listening to the radio chatter.

"Is it safe?" Egghead asked. "Or should we get the girls out of here first?"

Both Mandy and the pale girl turned to look at him. Mandy knew she was rolling her eyes, but she couldn't see the pale girl's. Shades? Wearing them in the bloody dusk of day?

"I carried your arse once, don't make me conk ya and carry ye wee bones outta here again, boyo," Mandy said, pulling his hand back from her cheek.

"I ... I mean ... you are ... just that I—"

Mandy leaned forward and kissed him on the forehead, rendering him mute.

"That works?" the pale girl asked.

"Seems to," Mandy told her. "Mandy," she said holding out her hand.

"Brooklyn," the pale girl said shaking her hand. "The tall

dude is McMinn, and it looks like you've met our Egghead here."

"Yeah, we've become a little acquainted in a short period of time, yeah?"

"Yeah," Egghead said, still three shades of red underneath the bruising.

They stayed there an hour, listening as the odd gunshot rang out. They were mostly in cover, but Brooklyn watched over things while Egghead and Mandy took turns cleaning each other's bumps and bruises from a kit she had. Mandy had long ago fixed her coverall situation and now that the fabric was drying, it was starting to stink and stick to her.

"Here's McMinn," Brooklyn said to them.

They struggled to their feet to see the smiling face of the tall man making his way toward them.

"We're all clear. All the CTS have been captured or … you know."

"I've done my fair share of killing them," Mandy told him.

"I know you have, but the others?" he shot back.

"I've got my own count, I'm sure," Mandy retorted. "Now if you blokes don't mind, I'm going to get my arse out of here. I have an island to return to, somehow."

"Going back to Dublin?" Egghead asked her suddenly.

"If I can make it," Mandy told him, then reached over and straightened his glasses.

He took it well, though everyone could see his ribs were hurting him. Finally, he leaned against the APC to take the weight off.

"McMinn, I almost forgot," Egbert said, pulling something from his pocket.

"What the bloody hell is that?" Mandy asked.

"Something that was earned because of a bloody hell.

Given to me by the man who earned it, which I then loaned to Egbert. It's a Purple Heart," McMinn said softly, holding his hand out as the medal was placed into it.

"Where did ye hide that from the guards?" Mandy asked Egbert, blurting the question out.

McMinn looked at the medal then back at the young man. "I'm going to need to use some *Purell* on my hands, aren't I?"

"No ..." Egghead stammered.

"Let's get out of here, kids," McMinn said standing up. "Ma'am, you're welcome to join us."

"Maybe I will for a time," Mandy said, getting under Egbert's shoulder on his hurt side. "But I've got places to be, and I want to make sure none of the CTS here lives."

"How bad was it?" Brooklyn asked.

"If you were a woman in there ..." She let the words trail off. "They were doing medical things. Something about fertility. I worry they were breeding the lasses here."

McMinn whispered something into the microphone on his vest. Gunshots started ringing out behind the building again. The air was thick with the stench of burning chemicals, burning buildings, burning bodies. Mandy saw him motion for them to start walking. She prayed no innocents were hurt in this breakout, but she was a realist. In every war, there were innocent lives lost. She'd done her best to send the CTS to hell. She just prayed she could find her way to a ship, a plane, some way back home.

"You could always stay here," Egghead told her softly as they walked.

"Maybe I will," she replied, grinning. "We'll see."

Together, they walked into the darkness, toward a rise of land where a group was waiting for them.

PART V: ARCHIE'S HEART

Written by P.A. Glaspy

31

Six Months Later

Archie looked around the barn at all of the patriots who had come together to fight for their lost freedom. The old building had been transformed into a barracks of sorts with people camped out in every available square foot. Tarps were scavenged and tacked to the walls to keep out the elements. It helped some.

Many people had spilled out into the paddock outside, and some had taken up residence in the farmhouse, having none of the reservations Archie had about it being seen as breaking and entering.

The medal that had started it all was assigned to a different young person to guard each day. Whoever had "Heart Duty" took pride in the assignment and showed great reverence to it and its original owner.

They looked to Archie as their leader. After all, the entire movement had started in his name. It wasn't a position he chose, but he didn't bear the burden of leadership alone. He had help. A lot of it.

Pockets of resistance across the state had become bigger

and bolder, taking on camps where prisoners had been used for harvesting their organs to sell to the highest bidder; where women were turned into breeding machines to keep the organ market fulfilled; where experiments were conducted on American children that no one could bring themselves to talk about. When these facilities were discovered, they were quickly taken out by whatever means was available to the resistance. And every time they took one down, they increased their ranks and their supplies.

The farmhouse had a large basement and a separate root cellar, both of which were crammed full of food stores, water purification systems, guns, ammo, and explosives. There was a cache of CTS uniforms that were used by Chinese Americans to infiltrate the camps and set the stage for the impending attack and subsequent liberation of those incarcerated. Their tactics were improving with every mission due in no small part to some of the people they had added to their ranks.

Roy Sterns had sought them out after the victory over the camp run by Dr. Huang, which had resulted in the loss of their commanding officer, Kyle Vanhorn. He brought along the remaining members of that group as well as supplies and vehicles. When they got there and found out that by either a stroke of luck or a guardian angel – or both – Archie was still alive, they took it as a sign they were where they needed to be. Roy had taken on an ever-growing militia group; Lyautey and Glaspy each commanded one as well.

McMinn had taken charge of the teens and was turning them into a mix of spies, scouts, scavengers and soldiers. He had given up trying to distance himself from them and decided to teach them the skills the resistance needed them to have. David was his second-in-command and was always keeping an eye on the new refugees who showed up almost daily for possible recruits. He watched for young people who had the spark of determination or were angry at the state of their world. Those were the best recruits.

All of the new arrivals were screened for any specific skillsets they might have, and everyone had to spend their first two weeks confined to a holding area so that they could be watched closely. Infiltrators had been discovered twice, and one of them was in the process of contacting his superiors when he was found out. McMinn dispatched the man and gave his radio to Jackie to monitor for any intel. Growing up in a bilingual home, Jackie could translate the Mandarin spoken on the radio and pass along anything important.

Dr. Valerie Fikes had found her family after the compound was taken down and they had joined the movement. She served as the camp physician and her husband, who had donated much of his free time to a soup kitchen before the invasion, took over the camp cooking. They had plenty of food that had been scavenged from the decimated camps; enough to last for the foreseeable future.

While the shot that was supposed to have ended Archie's life failed, it didn't leave him completely unscathed. He had been experiencing migraines, the icepick-stabbing-through-your-eye-into-your-brain variety, and when they hit, he was pretty much down for the count until it passed. While they had a good supply of pain medications in their stores, Archie refused them saying they should be used for someone who really needed them.

In a surprise move, Brooklyn took his left hand and pressed the space between the base of his left thumb and index finger. She applied pressure as she moved her own thumb in a circular motion on the spot. Within five minutes, Archie reported that the pain was greatly diminished. Valerie asked her what she had done.

"Acupressure. Like acupuncture but without the needles. My mom ..." her voice caught when she mentioned her mother. She took a deep breath and continued. "She used to get bad migraines and that's how Dad helped her. He taught me how and where to apply the pressure to help a lot of different things."

Valerie nodded and said, "I'd love it if you'd teach me. I think that might come in handy now. Would you do that?"

"Sure," Brooklyn said with a shrug. "I'll hit you up later. I'm late for training and Uncle Mick gets cranky when we're late. Feel better, Archie." She turned on her heels and hurried off, her white blonde ponytail swishing in time to her walk.

Valerie turned back to her patient. "What's your pain level now, Archie?"

Archie rotated his head in a circle. "I'd say about a three, Doc. Nothing I can't handle."

"Excellent. Let me know if it gets any worse. That acupressure treatment may only be a temporary pain reliever. We'll see. I need –"

A loud voice with a strong Irish accent interrupted Valerie.

"Are ya tryin' to blow us all to kingdom come, ya feckin' eejit? I don't know about you but I'm not in any hurry to meet the Man upstairs today! I said *gently* set it down!" Mandy's actions at the internment camp had landed her in charge of all things explosive-related and she was trying to teach some of the other young people how to do it. Not all of them took to it.

"Sorry, Mandy, it slipped," Scoop replied dejectedly.

"Well, that slip could have been the end of us all," she said, hands on her hips. "Now, watch closely as I show ya for the tenth feckin' time!"

Archie walked over to see what the commotion was about. Taking in the scene, he leaned over to Mandy and whispered, "Are they really working with live explosive materials?"

"Jay-sus, no, Arch," she whispered back. "We'd all have been at the pearly gates more than once by now if they were. But they don't know that. Thinkin' ya could kill yerself and everyone around ya tends to make people more careful." She looked at Scoop, whose hands were shaking worse than before as he tried to set the container down gently as instructed. "Most people anyway," she added, shaking her head.

Archie chuckled. "Carry on then." He made his way across the yard to where McMinn was working with a group of teens. The lesson today was apparently field stripping and cleaning weapons. They had a wide variety laid out on the tables in front of them. Archie peered over the shoulder of one of the kids.

"Missed a spot," he said softly. The boy jumped in surprise, as he hadn't heard Archie come up behind him. He peered closely at the slide he held in his hand, then wiped the whole piece down again. He looked up at Archie who gave him a wink and a pat on the shoulder as he continued on his way. He met McMinn who was making his rounds to check their progress, his dog, Shithead, at his heel.

"They're doing very well," Archie commented as he watched Brooklyn put the pistol she had cleaned back together as fast as any soldier he had ever seen.

McMinn nodded. "They're like sponges, soaking up everything I tell or teach them. I don't know if their dedication stems from boredom, a desire for revenge, or what, but I'll take it."

"I'd like to get the leaders together to go over OPSEC here, as well as start working on a plan to liberate any of the camps we find, say within fifty miles of us," Archie said. "If that goes well, we can expand further."

McMinn cocked his head at Archie. "Are you sure you want to bring any more attention to this place – well, any more than we're probably already getting with so many folks here now?"

Archie looked around at the place. There were pockets of people everywhere, working together to provide for the group: food, clothing, shelter; some teaching, others learning; he could hear one of the babies McMinn had rescued crying inside the farmhouse. He also heard people talking to each other, laughing, and acting normal; not having to hide anything from anyone. He hadn't realized how much he missed the sounds of normal.

He turned back to McMinn with a smile. "Yes, I'm sure. These people are living, really living, for the first time in a long time. I don't know how long it will last but I want to find as many more as we can and give them the chance to do the same."

"Well, I have no problem with more people. We've got plenty of Chinese guns. We need some bodies to use them. What's the word from town?"

"It looks like people all over the country are rallying together in groups like ours," Archie said. "The enemy is pulling back into the larger cities. I heard Texas is almost free of them. That movement is spreading through all of the surrounding states."

McMinn smirked as he replied, "I guess real Americans don't much give a rat's ass what the government decided to do. We kind of value our freedom and since we never gave them permission to give it away there's a bunch of us fighting to get it back."

"I'd say you're right. I don't think the Chinese counted on that. They are raised in a world where you do what you're told and don't question authority. We, on the other hand, don't like being told what to do. Our country was founded by people who wouldn't do as they were told."

"You've got that right," McMinn said. At the sound of

someone yelling, they both turned. Jackie was running toward them with the radio held aloft.

"Archie! Uncle Mick! Something's happening!" he shouted as he made his way to them. Everyone in the area started toward them as well to hear the news. Jackie skidded to a stop and leaned over with his hands on his knees trying to catch his breath.

"Slow down and stop calling me that!" McMinn barked at him. The crowd hid grins and snickers as they waited to hear what Jackie had to say. He stood up, took a couple of deep breaths and went on.

"They're abandoning the camps!" Jackie got out between gasps.

Everyone started talking at once. "Quiet!" McMinn shouted. When the crowd had settled down, he went on. "What do you mean? Are they releasing everyone?"

Jackie was shaking his head. "No! The soldiers and commanders are leaving and they're keeping the people locked up. Some of them are planning to set the camp they're responsible for on fire!"

Archie and McMinn looked at each other as the crowd started shouting. Leaning in, Archie said, "Leadership meeting. Now."

32

THE PLAN WAS SIMPLE.

Go to the first camp, clean house if needed, free the people. Rinse and repeat at the next one. Try to get at least two in a day.

Unfortunately, it wasn't that simple.

At the first camp they attacked, they were met with heavy resistance. They sustained casualties and at least a dozen wounded. Apparently, their commander hadn't gotten the memo to abandon ship – or didn't care. Mandy's explosives gave them an advantage, taking out most of the soldiers and towers, but it seemed the commander had some explosives of his own. He stood in the center of the yard screaming in broken English while holding up a remote detonator switch.

"You surrender, or I blow up barracks! All the people die! You lose!"

Archie called out, "*You* surrender, comrade, and we'll let you live! You kill those people, you will definitely die!"

The man seemed to be considering Archie's counteroffer. Archie decided to sweeten the pot. "Put the detonator down and you can walk out of here and go wherever you want.

We've got the place surrounded and you are totally outnumbered. We don't want anyone else to die. We just want our people freed."

The commander stood there a moment longer, then gave a curt nod indicating his agreement to the terms. He slowly set the detonator on the ground. He returned to an upright position and raised his hands. The sound of the rifle firing and the man's head snapping backward happened simultaneously. A spray of blood and brain matter preceded his fall to the ground.

Showing no surprise, Archie looked up at the sniper on top of one of the armored vehicles they had commandeered from a previous enemy camp. McMinn ejected the spent casing and, still looking at the man he had just killed, replied, "No prisoners. No mercy."

Staring at the corpse, Archie said, "Agreed."

Roy led his team through the gates and cleared the yard, then proceeded to the barracks followed by the rest of the group, leaving a security detail posted. Chains were cut, and the doors thrown open wide. Dazed and confused, the occupants came out slowly. Seeing the commander lying in a pool of his own blood, they started a cheer that soon reverberated throughout the camp. The former captives hugged their saviors and many cried tears of joy and relief.

One young woman looked up at Archie and whispered, "Is it over? Can we go home now?"

Archie took in her appearance. The camp clothes she wore were dirty and torn, as if she had been attacked. Her face was scarred, lacerations that should have been stitched left to heal as they were. Her hair was matted, and she smelled as if she hadn't been allowed to bathe for quite some time. Paying no heed to the filth, Archie placed an arm around her shoulders and steered her toward the transport vehicles. Softly, he whispered, "We're taking you to a new home."

The scavenger teams made short work of gathering supplies from the camp stores. The bedding in the barracks was beyond horrific, so they stuck with the storage buildings. Institutional style clothing would be taken back and modified to be serviceable without reminding the wearer of what they were before. All food, guns, and ammo were taken, including guns from dead combatants. If they could use it to fight or survive, they took it. Some of the former captives even helped them load the trucks, eager to assist in any way the people who had freed them from a slow, yet certain death.

McMinn and Mandy had checked the barracks and found they were indeed wired with C4. They carefully removed the detonators and gathered the bricks of explosives to take back with them. Mandy was particularly pleased with the acquisition.

"At least those muppets can handle this stuff and I'll not have ta worry that they'll be accidentally blowing something up. Or someone. Or themselves, truth be told."

McMinn shook his head and replied, "Some of them aren't ever going to be good at it and they shouldn't have to. They're kids, for God's sake. They're not supposed to have to know how to handle explosives and shit like that. They should be going out on dates and playing video games and taking selfies and putting those stupid filters on them. All that ridiculous crap teenagers used to do. Not learning how to kill people and scavenging for food."

Mandy patted him on the arm. "I hear ya, Mick, and I agree but what's done is done. This is the world we have now, so we have to learn to live in this one. We've got a sayin' in my country: *You've got to do your own growing, no matter how tall yer father was.* What our parents had – what we had – is in the past. We've all got to figure out what we're supposed to do now, what we should be doing to get along. I'm not much older than these kiddos but I grew up way different than them. I don't think many of them have had to struggle or work for anything in their lives. I just hope we can teach them what they need to know to make it in *this* world. Because no matter what happens from here on out, the old one is gone for good."

"It doesn't make it suck any less ... for them."

"Or us," Mandy added.

With everything they wanted to take loaded on the trucks, all of the buildings were doused with gasoline as they made their way back through the camp and headed out of the gates. Once outside them, the last vehicle stopped so that four men and women could hurry back to the closest buildings, usually the commander's office and a guard shack, and set them ablaze. The buildings were close enough that the fire jumped from one to the next until the entire complex was burning.

With satisfied smiles, the rebels drove away.

33

AFTER DROPPING the refugees off at the farm, the group went to the next camp on their list. Their elation at their success from the last one turned to devastation and grief at the next. The camp was gone, every building torched, with piles of burned bodies in the yard. They could still feel the heat of the blaze in the air and see wispy tendrils of smoke rising from everything. It seemed at this camp the commander had ordered the captives executed, piled the corpses up and set them on fire. There was no one left alive, no supplies to commandeer, no resistance to deal with. The place was a burned-out husk, barely resembling what it had been before.

"Animals! Feckin' animals the whole lot of 'em!" Mandy cried from the lead truck. "We're too late, Mick!"

McMinn stepped out of the passenger side door and walked to the open gate. There was no reason for the Chinese to have locked it behind them. There was nothing left to contain or protect. Archie joined him, and the two former soldiers stared at the rubble and charred remains.

"Such a waste," Archie said quietly. "All those lives sacrificed. Why?"

"No good reason. Just because they could." McMinn's voice was laced with anger. "Just so you know, I plan on killing every one of those sons of bitches I find."

"I'm good with that," Archie replied.

They loaded everyone back up and headed out for the next camp on their list. McMinn was looking at a map with the known locations marked. He caught a movement out of the corner of his eye in the tree line to his right. Turning his head slightly he saw what appeared to be Chinese soldiers running through the woods. He turned fully and peered through a set of binoculars. What had looked like Chinese because of the uniforms they wore were actually Americans. McMinn told Scoop, who was driving, to stop. The rest of the caravan pulled in behind them. McMinn jumped out and looked again. Then he called out.

"Hey! We're not Chinese! We're American like you! We can help you!"

The runners slowed down but didn't come out of hiding. One of them yelled back, "How do we know you aren't working with them, or that you won't turn us in to the next patrol you see for extra food rations?"

McMinn hesitated a moment.

Mandy took the opportunity to enter the exchange. "Because we're driving their feckin' trucks as you can see and killin' every one of the bastards we find! They don't give a rat's arse about us rebels. C'mon now – let us take ya somewhere safe. Well, safer than out here!"

No one moved at first, then a young lady came out of the trees and started toward them. The man with her grabbed her arm trying to keep her there, but she snatched it away from him.

"I'm tired, Jimmy! Tired of running, hiding, eating bugs and sleeping in the dirt! I don't care if they *are* spies. I'm done!" She continued toward them at a slow but steady pace and seemed to be limping.

When she got to the truck, it was apparent to everyone waiting that she had been out in the elements for a while. Though pulled back in a ponytail, her hair was ratty and oily. The uniform she was wearing was filthy and had tears in both knees which were also covered in dried, crusted blood. She had cuts and scrapes on her exposed forearms as well as across most of her face. She looked like hell.

McMinn addressed her in a kind but firm tone. "We're going to have to search you, miss. For all we know, *you* could be a spy."

She laughed out loud. "If I could be a spy then they treat their spies even shittier than their prisoners. We stole these uniforms from the laundry they had us working in. When everything started coming apart, we escaped. But, sure, go ahead and search me, mister."

He motioned for Mandy to conduct the procedure and she made short work of it.

"No weapons and she's skin and bones. C'mon ... uh, what's yer name, lass?"

"Stacy."

"Nice to meet ya, Stacy. I'm Mandy. This tall fella here is McMinn, but we all call him Mick. Now, let's get you something to eat."

She took her back to the vehicle Archie was riding in which held a lot of their food and water for traveling. She introduced Stacy to Archie then slid the side door on the van open. Egbert looked up at them and smiled.

"Hey Mandy! Who's your friend?"

"This is Stacy, Eggie, and she needs some food. The poor girl is skin and bones. Stacy, this is Egbert, but he also answers to Egghead, Eggie, and muppet." She grinned at him on the last one.

Egbert shook his head and opened a plastic container. He pulled out a biscuit with a piece of fried Spam in it. He handed it to Stacy, along with a water bottle.

"Here you go, Stacy. The biscuits are made with powdered milk, so you might detect that taste and we have a lot of Spam. I hope that's okay."

Stacy took the biscuit and ate it in four bites. She drank half the bottle of water and exclaimed, "Oh my – that was heaven. I ate crickets yesterday. Tried to eat a worm but I just couldn't do it. That was as good as a steak to me right now. Thank you!"

He handed her another one. "You shouldn't eat too much if you've been going without for a while, but I think one more won't hurt."

She took the proffered biscuit, turned to her friends still in the woods, held it up and called out, "Biscuits! I'm eating biscuits! They have *real* food and clean water! Get over here!"

They hurried out of hiding and after each was searched, they were given food and water. There were ten in all, most in the same condition as Stacy.

"Looks like this wasn't a bust after all," Archie said as they watched the new people become more animated with each bite.

"Yep, I'd call this a secondary win," McMinn replied. "I think we can go home for now, Archie."

"Sounds good to me."

Mandy rode back to the rebel camp in the van Egbert was driving with Stacy and Jimmy. They shared their internment stories with each other. Stacy had experienced similar treatment to Mandy's, so they had that in common. When Mandy told them the story of her wild exit, they stared at her wide-eyed.

"You blew the place up? And strangled the overseer with wire and pencils?" Jimmy said in awe. "Are you like a secret agent or something?"

Mandy grinned, while Egbert guffawed from the front. Mandy smacked him in the back of the head. Satisfied with the "Ow!" she received, she went on.

"Nah, nothin' like that. Just grew up in a rough place and learned a few things."

"All we did was steal some uniforms and sneak out when everything went to hell," Stacy replied.

"And that's pretty impressive, too," Mandy said. "If you hadn't, you wouldn't be here right now. The rest of the folks from the camp you were at are dead."

Stacy's hand moved quickly to cover her mouth, stifling an outcry. Jimmy put an arm around her shoulder. She leaned over and cried silent tears into his chest.

"Her best friend was in there," Jimmy explained softly. "We tried to get her to come with us, but she was too scared."

Mandy nodded sadly. "Sorry for your loss, lass. Tis troubled times we're in right now, that's for sure. But at least some of you made it out alive."

They pulled up to the farm and Mandy watched as their eyes grew wider when they saw it.

"All these people were freed from camps?" Jimmy asked.

"Most, not all. Some of us never got caught in the first place and hid out wherever we could. I was one of them," Egbert replied.

Egbert parked the van and they all piled out. Valerie was outside attending to the refugees brought earlier and came over.

"Hello! I'm Dr. Fikes, but everyone calls me Valerie or Doc. I answer to both." She smiled at them as she took in each face, then said, "Does anyone need medical attention?

You all look to be in much better shape than the last group that arrived, but just thought I'd check."

One of the girls stepped forward. "Hi, Doc. I might have sprained my wrist yesterday. I don't think it's broke, but it hurts like hell." She held her left arm out which had lots of bruising around the wrist area.

Valerie went to her and started moving the hand around. "What's your name, sweetie?"

"Tonya."

Tonya flinched more than once as Valerie manipulated the joint. "Yes, I believe you're right. Come with me and we'll get that wrapped up. It's funny but sometimes a sprain is more painful than a break." She ushered the girl to the pop-up awning she was using as a triage area. A couple of others followed them.

Archie had joined the group by then. "I hope you understand but we need to quarantine you all for a few days. It's just a precaution to make sure everybody is who they say they are, and no one has a hidden agenda. You'll be given food and water, shelter and clean clothes. You'll be kept under guard and restricted to one specific area. Once we're sure you aren't a spy, you'll be allowed to join the rest of our little community and we'll help you find the right job to suit your skills. Does anyone have a problem with that?"

Everyone shook their heads indicating they didn't and most of them looked relieved. One of the young men spoke up, confirming that suspicion.

"No, sir, that's just fine. I for one am just happy to see free Americans again!"

Archie smiled at him. McMinn stepped up. "Y'all follow me and I'll show you where you're gonna be bunking for now."

McMinn headed for an area of the grounds that had been set up with large military tents, confiscated in previous raids, and nothing more than a police crime scene tape roping it off. Two men and two women manned the four corners. McMinn acknowledged them with a nod of his head as he ducked under the tape then held it up for those following him. Many of the people they had liberated earlier were already there milling about the yard. Once everyone was inside the perimeter, he pointed to the tents.

"Left for the women, right for the men. You'll find cots and bedding inside. If you're married or even just a couple, you'll need to go to your designated tent. We can't accommodate you staying together here. Once your quarantine is over, we'll help you set up your permanent shelter. As you can see, privacy is not something we have a lot of but we're kind of a big family here. Latrines are out back; showers, too. One of guards will escort you no more than two at a time. Sorry for the internment camp feel, but we've been burned before, and we have to do what we can to keep everyone safe."

They were looking around at the indicated facilities and peeking inside the tents. The young man who had spoken earlier said, "Who did all this? I mean, this place wasn't set up like this before the invasion, right?"

"We all did. It's grown over time. When we got here ... oh, I guess it was about six months ago ... it was just the house, that old barn and fields. We've been liberating the smaller camps for a while now. We brought the people and any supplies we thought we could use back here. We have quite a few vets with us and if there's one thing an old soldier can do it's dig a latrine and set up a base camp. Everybody pitches in."

"Whose place is this?" another young man asked. "Is the owner here, too?"

McMinn shrugged. "No idea. They aren't here, never have been that I know of. Archie found the place and set up in the barn not too long after the invasion. He has a pretty amazing story that a lot of people here have played a part in. Maybe he'll share it with you."

A small girl spoke softly. "Are we safe here? It's kind of out in the open. What about the Chinese? I don't want to go to another camp. I can't, I just can't." Tears were streaming down her face as she spoke.

"From the intelligence we've gathered, they're giving up on smaller communities like ours and pulling back to the big cities. I guess we're more trouble than we're worth." McMinn grinned mischievously at the frightened girl. She looked back at him with a shy smile.

"Thank you! Thank you so much for taking us in! We'll do whatever we need to do to help out," she replied. "Just tell us where to start."

"For now, just rest up and we'll get some food in you in a bit. If anyone wants to shower, it's lukewarm if the sun's been out, and cold if it hasn't, but clean is better than dirty in my book. Someone will be here shortly with towels and clothes. Excuse me." McMinn turned to leave and found Archie standing there waiting for him. They walked together across the yard.

"You think they're who they say they are?" Archie asked when they were a safe distance away.

McMinn nodded and said, "Yeah, my gut tells me they're too scared to be spies. They're still going to be kept separate from the rest of the camp for now. No sense taking a chance that my gut is wrong for once."

"Agreed. Let's get something to eat."

The new arrivals were in good spirits having eaten, showered and changed into clean clothes. They were standing outside the tents taking in the sights of the camp. Stacy noticed one of the guys in their group, Dennis, was vigorously scratching at his left forearm. She went over to him and saw that he had dug deep gashes into it with his nails.

"Dennis, what's wrong with your arm? Did you get into some poison ivy or something when we were in the woods?"

"Nah, it was itching before at the camp. That Chinese doctor kept telling me it was hives and put numbing cream on it every day. It kept it from itching, but I haven't had any for a couple of days and it's driving me crazy now!" He continued digging at the spot on his arm.

"You better go see the doc. Maybe she has some of that cream," Stacy said.

"Yeah, I guess so." Dennis went to one of the people standing guard. "I think I need to see the doc about my arm."

The young man looked at it and seeing the angry welts called out to a teen walking by.

"Hailey, can you go get the doc? Tell her it's a very itchy arm thing."

Hailey smiled and called back, "You've got it! B-R-B!"

They all chuckled at her use of the acronym for *Be Right Back* normally reserved for texting. After a few minutes, Hailey came back with Valerie, carrying what looked like a small tackle box.

"Hi, I'm Dr. Fikes. What seems to be the problem?"

Dennis held his arm out to her. She took a look at the irritated area on his arm, then reached into the box and pulled out gauze and alcohol. She dampened the gauze and looked at the young man's face.

"How long has it been like this? This is going to sting, by the way." She cleaned the area which caused him to flinch. "Sorry about that. What's your name?"

"Dennis. It's been like that for a few weeks."

"And the other doctor said it was hives?" Having cleared the blood away she was now peering at the spot and gently touching it.

"Yeah, like a reaction to the needle they used."

She paused and looked up at him. "What was the needle for?"

He shrugged and replied, "They took some blood for some tests and there was like a lump there afterwards and he said I must've had a reaction to the needle."

"They took blood from your forearm, not the bend of your elbow?" she asked, a note of concern in her voice.

"Um, yeah ... why? Is something wrong?" Now Dennis sounded worried.

"I'm not sure." She turned to Hailey. "Go get McMinn and Archie and bring them here. Now."

34

"He's got a tracker of some kind in his arm," she told them in a low voice when she met them a few steps away from the group.

"Shit," McMinn replied. "I guess my gut *was* wrong this time. They're leading somebody here."

Valerie shook her head. "I don't think he knows it's there. The Chinese doctor fed him a bunch of BS about a reaction to a needle and then kept it numbed."

"Can you take it out?" Archie asked.

"Yes, but I'm sure the damage is done." She looked scared. "Should we get out of here?"

"I'm not sure where we would go, and I have no idea how to move this many people and all of the supplies we've gathered. I don't know about you but I'm tired of hiding in my own country. Besides, I'm supposed to be dead already. I have no problem dying right here." Archie's voice, full of resolve, ended strong and his statement had an air of finality to it.

"I'm good with that," McMinn replied. "I still want that tracker out of him. Let's make that happen ASAP."

Valerie nodded and went back to the group. Archie and

McMinn knew exactly when she told Dennis what was causing the irritation to his arm.

"What? A tracker? Get it out! Get it out now!" he yelled.

Valerie called out to the two men. "Can you escort him to the triage tent? I'll need more equipment than what I have with me."

Archie and McMinn went to her and motioned for the young man to follow them. As they were walking, Dennis cried, "I'm sorry! I didn't know! They told me it was a knot under the skin. I swear!"

"We know," Archie replied. "We're about to get it out of you. Just hold on."

They walked to the triage area together. McMinn stopped at the edge and said, "Try not to destroy it, Doc. I've got plans for it."

She gave him a nod and went to work. Once she had extracted it, she rinsed it with water and handed it to him. "What are you going to do with it?"

"Take it back where it came from."

Dr. Huang watched the screen showing the little flashing dot indicating the location of the man they had implanted with the transmitter. When the dot disappeared, he shouted, "Mark that location! They've discovered the tracking device. That's where we want to strike!"

"Shall we order the missile launch, Doctor?" the young captain attending him asked.

"Yes! Attack! We will rid ourselves of that pesky rebel group once and for all!"

35

When McMinn told them where he was going and why, Hailey, Brooklyn, and David asked to accompany him. There were enough people at their camp now to provide security without them having to be in the mix.

They were taking the van Egbert had driven earlier when they picked up the last group. Archie walked with them to the van. Looking inside, he told McMinn, "You should get some extra supplies. It's getting dark soon and you may not get back tonight. You should always have food and water with you for at least a week."

"Yeah, we didn't get it restocked after that last group. They put a pretty good dent in what was here." McMinn spoke to the kids. "You guys go get a week's supply of food and water for each of us." They hurried off to do as he had requested. Shithead stayed with McMinn, anticipating a ride and not wanting to be left behind.

When they were alone, Archie said, "We may not have much longer here, Mick. That tracker was like an arrow overhead pointing straight down at us. I was serious about not leaving but some of the people may want to try to make a go of it somewhere else. We should probably have a group meeting when you get back. We can let everyone know about our concerns and make sure they know they can set out on their own or even with others if they don't feel safe here."

"Sounds good, Arch. I doubt many of them will want to head out of here though. This is a pretty good setup, especially at a time like this. Food, water, shelter, some semblance of freedom – it's the best we've had in a while."

The kids were coming back laden with gallon jugs of water, canned meats, crackers, a case of MREs and Pop Tarts. McMinn shook his head. "Nice balanced diet you planned for us."

Brooklyn set her load in the back of the van, then turned back to the two older men. "We probably won't eat any of it anyway. From what you said, the camp isn't that far. At most, we can have Vienna sausages and crackers with Pop Tarts for dessert. Sounds tasty to me."

Archie chuckled. "Yes, a well-rounded meal for sure. I still find it strange they had so many Pop Tarts."

David deposited his load. "Toaster pastries filled with a mysterious berry substance, topped with icing and sprinkles – what's not to love?"

"Alright, let's get moving. Load up, people," McMinn said gruffly. Archie watched them pull out then headed back toward the center of camp.

As Archie was passing the triage tent, Valerie spoke.

"Have you got a minute, Archie?"

He changed direction and walked over to her. "Sure, Doc. What's up?"

Hesitantly, she replied, "Are you sure we're going to be okay here?"

Archie nodded slowly. "I think so, but we're going to have a group meeting when McMinn gets back to talk over options for everyone. Of course, not everyone knows what we know, but they will at the meeting. No one has to stay if they're uncomfortable or worried about being discovered here."

Relief shown on her face. "Oh, good. I look forward to it. I really want to stay."

Archie smiled at her. "We really want you to, Valerie. See you later." He turned and walked toward the barn.

Suddenly, he heard a familiar sound. One he hadn't heard since he was deployed. He knew that sound. It was one that chilled him to his very core. He looked up and saw the incoming missile.

There was no time. No time to run. No time to hide. No time to pray for the miracle they needed.

He closed his eyes and whispered, "I die free."

36

David drove while McMinn provided directions and kept an eye out for potential threats. They were on their way back to the camp that had been burned. McMinn wanted to leave a message for the Chinese. He had placed the tracking device in a small cardboard box then wrapped aluminum foil around it to block the signal until the last minute. Once they got there, he had a nice surprise cooked up by Mandy to attach the tracker to which would detonate as soon as it was picked up.

About a mile away from their base camp, they heard an unfamiliar sound. McMinn rolled the window down. He stuck his head out to look up.

A shiver ran down his spine and filled him with dread.

"Dear God – that's a missile! And it's headed for the farm!"

David slammed on the brakes and quickly pulled over so that they could all get out to see what was going on. They watched as the missile made its decent then stared in horror at the huge fireball that went up.

The explosion shook the ground even though they were a mile away.

Shithead was running from person to person, barking and howling, somehow sensing that danger was near. McMinn grabbed his collar, squatted down, and wrapped his arms around the dog to calm him.

"Come on! We've got to go back! Get in!" David yelled.

The kids piled into the van, screaming and crying, as McMinn tried to yell over the cacophony.

"Guys!"

No response.

"Hey! Listen to me!"

They ignored him, caught up in their fear and grief at the potential loss of those they had come to care for.

Throwing Shithead up into the floorboard, McMinn reached across the van, stopping David from turning the wheel to go back the direction they had come.

He swallowed hard, his hand firmly holding the wheel. "It's too late. There's no way *anyone* lived through that. Just drive. I don't want your last memories of them to be what we'd find back there."

Brooklyn released a mournful wail from the back. Shithead crawled between the front seats to reach her and added his own howl to hers.

David laid his head on the steering wheel, sobbing softly.

McMinn tossed the tracker out the window and looked at Hailey, who had tears streaming down her cheeks as she gently touched the medal pinned to her chest. It was her day to guard the Purple Heart. In that moment, he made a decision.

"Head southeast. Somebody's getting a damn happy ending here. We're going to Tennessee."

Brooklyn burst up between the seats. "No! I'm not leaving until we know for sure! Go back! We have to see for ourselves if there are any survivors. I'll walk back if I have to!"

McMinn closed his eyes and took a deep breath. When he didn't speak, Hailey reached up and gently touched his shoulder.

"Please, Uncle Mick, can we just go back and check first? Please?"

Though he pretended it irritated him, the nickname the kids had given him endeared them to him even more. He cared about them.

But these kids hadn't seen war. Not real war. And he didn't want them to, not if he could keep it from them. It's one thing to see strangers executed, bodies burned beyond recognition.

It's another thing entirely when it's people you know and love.

His mind was playing images of devastation and horror like an old war movie except his friends were the ghastly stars.

He didn't want to see it either.

Yet, he'd watched these kids mature under his guidance. It wouldn't be right to leave them always wondering *what if* ...

No, they had to see for themselves or they'd never be able to accept their friend's deaths. He had no doubt it would haunt them for the rest of their days, just as his own visions did from war; scenes that still haunted his dreams at night. But they needed the closure.

With a loud exhale, he nodded to David. "Alright. Go back," he mumbled. He rubbed a hand over his face, trying to scrub away the scene he knew was waiting for them there. The scene that was already playing out in his mind.

David gunned the engine and hurried back toward the farm, a dust cloud billowing up behind them.

They turned the corner and as one breathed a sigh of relief.

The camp was a beehive of activity.

David skidded to a stop and they jumped out, running to Archie who stood in the middle of the chaos, shouting directions and pointing his arms this way and that.

Shithead ran to Egbert, nearly knocking the boy down, then to Archie, and one by one the rest of his "pack" … seeming to know they had dodged a bullet – a big one.

The refuges and rebels alike were frantically working together, standing in a line passing supplies from one person to the next. The gear was being thrown into one pile, tents torn down and thrown into another, and the food was being packed into wagons.

In another pile was a fast-growing stack of backpacks and burlap sacks, which were being stuffed and loaded into cars, wheelbarrows, and onto the backs of anyone who could carry them.

McMinn stepped out of the van, waving smoke away from his eyes in disbelief. A half-mile past the farm, the woods were on fire, and the flames stretched from the treetops into the sky, like hell on earth.

The missile had missed the camp.

Barely.

He hurried over to Archie. "Are you okay? I can't believe it missed!"

"Me either, Mick," Archie said in a shaky voice. "Glad it did though. And yeah, I'm good, just a loud ringing in my ears."

"So, where are we going now?" McMinn asked as he watched the frenzied activity around them.

Archie shrugged. "No idea. You lead, we'll follow."

McMinn shook his head. "Oh, no. This is *your* show. This whole thing started because of you."

Hailey approached them slowly, then ran in and hugged Archie, squeezing him tightly around his waist and burying her face against him. She let go and stepped back, swiping away tears of relief.

"He's right, Archie. *You're* the hero. I've got the proof right here."

She held her fist out and when it opened, the Purple Heart lay in her small palm. Archie reached over and picked up the symbol that had spawned a movement of people to fight for and regain their freedom.

With a sly smile, he replied, "Let's go find a new home."

ABOUT THE AUTHORS

Want to read more from the authors?

Archie, Part I, and *Archie's Heart*, Part V, by P.A. Glaspy

Click here to sign up to P.A. Glaspy's newsletter.

A.R.C.H.I.E., Part II, by L. Douglas Hogan

Click here to sign up to L. Douglas Hogan's newsletter.

Ditch of the Dead, Part III, by L.L. Akers

Click here to sign up to L.L. Akers' newsletter.

Mandy's Revenge, Part IV, by Boyd Craven III

Click here to sign up to Boyd Craven's newsletter.

Cover design by RicherDesigns.net

Want to find out more about the DD12 Reader's Group?

Archie, Part One of the *Archie's Heart* novel, Copyright © 2018 by P.A. Glaspy.

A.R.C.H.I.E., Part Two of the *Archie's Heart* novel, Copyright © 2018 by L. Douglas Hogan.

Ditch of the Dead, Part Three of the *Archie's Heart* novel, Copyright © 2018 by L.L. Akers.

Mandy's Revenge, Part Four of the *Archie's Heart* novel, Copyright © 2018 by Boyd Craven III.

Archie's Heart, Part Five of the *Archie's Heart* novel, Copyright © 2018 by P.A. Glaspy.

All rights reserved. Printed in the United States of America, First Release & Printing 2018

Please do not share this e-book. **It is against the law.** This book or any portion thereof may *not* be reproduced, scanned or distributed in any printed or electronic form without permission, or used in any manner whatsoever without the express written permission of the publisher, except for the use of brief quotations in a book review.

This is a work of fiction. Names, characters, businesses, places, events and incidents are either the products of the author's imagination or used in a fictitious manner. Any resemblance to actual persons, dead or living, business establishments, events or locales is coincidental.